W9-BZU-128

WISHING CASWELL DEAD

WISHING CASWELL DEAD

PAT STOLTEY

FIVE STAR
A part of Gale, a Cengage Company

GALE
A Cengage Company

Farmington Hills, Mich • San Francisco • New York • Waterville, Maine
Meriden, Conn • Mason, Ohio • Chicago

Copyright © 2017 by Patricia Stoltey
All scripture quotations, unless otherwise noted, are taken from the King James Bible.
Five Star™ Publishing, a part of Gale, a Cengage Company

ALL RIGHTS RESERVED.
This novel is a work of fiction. Names, characters, places, and incidents are either the product of the author's imagination, or, if real, used fictitiously.

No part of this work covered by the copyright herein may be reproduced or distributed in any form or by any means, except as permitted by U.S. copyright law, without the prior written permission of the copyright owner.

The publisher bears no responsibility for the quality of information provided through author or third-party Web sites and does not have any control over, nor assume any responsibility for, information contained in these sites. Providing these sites should not be construed as an endorsement or approval by the publisher of these organizations or of the positions they may take on various issues.

LIBRARY OF CONGRESS CATALOGING-IN-PUBLICATION DATA

Names: Stoltey, Patricia, author.
Title: Wishing Caswell dead / Pat Stoltey.
Description: First edition. | Waterville, Maine : Five Star Publishing, a part of Cengage Learning, Inc., [2017]
Identifiers: LCCN 2017022958 (print) | LCCN 2017026815 (ebook) | ISBN 9781432834388 (ebook) | ISBN 143283438X (ebook) | ISBN 9781432837075 (ebook) | ISBN 1432837079 (ebook) | ISBN 9781432834401 (hardcover) ISBN 1432834401 (hardcover)
Subjects: | GSAFD: Mystery fiction.
Classification: LCC PS3619.T6563 (ebook) | LCC PS3619.T6563 W57 2017 (print) | DDC 813/.6—dc23
LC record available at https://lccn.loc.gov/2017022958

First Edition. First Printing: December 2017
Find us on Facebook–https://www.facebook.com/FiveStarCengage
Visit our website–http://www.gale.cengage.com/fivestar/
Contact Five Star™ Publishing at FiveStar@cengage.com

Printed in the United States of America
1 2 3 4 5 6 7 21 20 19 18 17

In memory of my mom
Sylvia T. Swartz
May 10, 1919–December 27, 2016
and
For Raintree Writers
because they are the ones who kept this novel alive.

ACKNOWLEDGMENTS

Thank you with all my heart to the members of Raintree Writers, past and present, who reviewed and critiqued earlier versions of this novel.

As always, I am grateful to my editor, Deni Dietz, and to Five Star/Cengage for their continuing help and support.

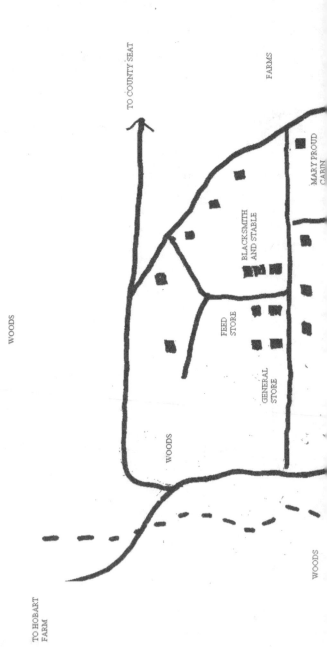

Village of Sangamon
State of Illinois
1834 Population 127

WOODS

WOODS

WOODS

WOODS

TO COUNTY SEAT

FARMS

TO HOBART FARM

FEED STORE

GENERAL STORE

BLACKSMITH AND STABLE

MARY PROUD CABIN

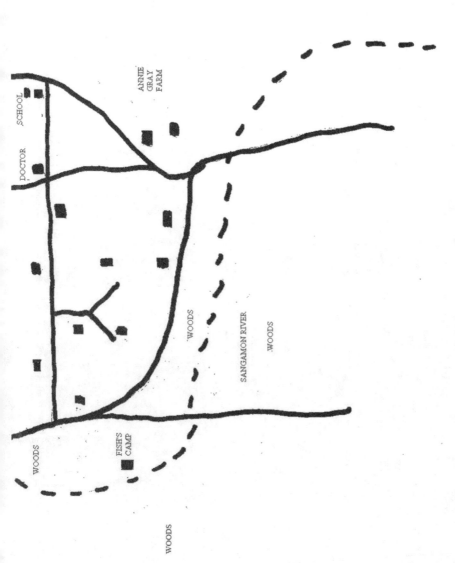

FARMS

WOODS

ANNIE
GRAY
FARM

SCHOOL

DOCTOR

WOODS

FISH'S
CAMP

WOODS

SANGAMON RIVER

WOODS

PROLOGUE:
SANGAMON VILLAGE, STATE OF ILLINOIS, APRIL 1834
THE BODY BY THE RIVER

"You sure he's dead?" asked Jeremiah Frost, owner of the general store.

"Ah, *oui*," Henri de Montagne answered, his accent even more pronounced than usual. "*Sans doubt.* His t'roat is . . ." The old trapper made a slashing motion across his neck. "The body sit against a tree . . ." He stopped, stared at the ground, and shook his head as though he could not think of any words to describe the scene in the woods.

"Well," said the saloonkeeper, "can't say we'll miss the boy, but he does need a proper burial."

"Aye," Jeremiah said. "Fetch a couple more men, maybe the smithy and his brother."

"I'll get them. And I'll go with you to the woods."

"Walk carefully when you reach the tree," warned Henri. "There's a nest of rattlers . . ." He crossed himself and mounted his sorrel mare.

"You going to show us where he is?" Jeremiah asked the trapper.

"*Mais non.*" Henri pointed toward the west. "I must go." As he backed his horse away from Jeremiah, he held his hand up as though to ward off the protests.

"The law won't take kindly to him rushing off like that," the saloonkeeper muttered.

"Nothing to be said for it," Jeremiah answered.

Henri dug his heels into his horse's flank and slapped its

11

neck with the reins. The horse galloped away with Henri hunched forward and two reluctant mules dragged in its dusty wake.

Jeremiah and the other three men from Sangamon entered the overgrown woods to search for the body. Colin Pritchard, the blacksmith, carried a sheet, rolled and tucked under his arm. Jeremiah held his musket ready and, at the same time, held on to his horse's reins, pulling him along in case he needed to mount in a hurry. Neither precaution gave him comfort. The others had left their horses a few feet away, but glanced back often once they realized Jeremiah had not done the same. They approached the river, creeping toward the willow tree as though they feared the dead man would hear their footsteps.

They found the body at the bend in the Sangamon River, propped against the tree just as they'd been told. Undisturbed by scavengers. Staring wide-eyed and open-mouthed toward the river where the weeping willow dangled its yellow-green whips over the muddy waters.

The four men stood in a ragged line and gawked, taking in the body's mangled throat, the pallor of Caswell Proud's face, the blood-soaked shirt.

The day was warm and clear, but the canopy of branches and vines, bursting with spring buds and baby leaves, filtered the sun and cloaked the woods in shadows. Each snapping twig, nervous cough, and cleared throat was sucked into the silence. Jeremiah tried to take a deep breath but failed. He forced a yawn but it did not satisfy his need for air.

Jeremiah trembled and searched the shadows, starting at every tiny movement in the brush. His uneasiness was not about Caswell's death. That taken alone was not all bad. It was the future that had Jeremiah spooked. The unmentionable secret that ticked away in his gut, the secret that might blow his life apart if the law showed up to ask questions about the murdered Caswell Proud, and if Caswell's mother or sister decided to give truthful answers.

His horse seemed to sense his mood and skittered sideways at the sound of some tiny critter speeding through the leaves and branches on the ground. Jeremiah tore his gaze away from the body, pulled on the reins to draw the horse closer, and patted him on the neck.

"Bring that sheet on up here," he said. "Let's be done with this."

The smithy unrolled the cloth and stretched it out on the ground alongside the dead man. "We going to bury him in the town cemetery, Jeremiah?"

"Don't much like that idea. Folks got to agree, and I reckon most would object." Jeremiah mounted his horse and watched as the others wrapped the body, tucking in the edges so it would remain covered when they entered the town. Jeremiah led the way as they carried Caswell Proud through the woods to the clearing where the other horses were tethered. Nobody had anything to say as they strapped the body to a makeshift travois.

On the trip back to Sangamon, Jeremiah thought about the murder of Caswell Proud. He'd seen the results of violence before, but knowing who'd been involved in a quarrel and who hated the victim enough to kill him convinced a community no one else was in danger. Here, with this murder, things were more complicated. No one simple dispute, but a long history of insults and invasions. No one single suspect, but maybe a hundred folks with secrets as bad as Jeremiah's. And a victim so despicable maybe God himself had decided to take a swipe at cleaning up his garden along the Sangamon River.

CHAPTER ONE:
SANGAMON VILLAGE,
NINE MONTHS EARLIER,
JULY 1833
JO MAE PROUD

I mostly had one thing I thought about every minute of my life until the day I left Sangamon. *If I have anything to say about it, Caswell will go to hell, and the sooner the better.* And from time to time, I even had it in my mind to help my wishes along a bit.

Caswell was my big brother, and you know how a girl always wishes she had a big brother to look out for her and beat off the bullies and snakes and mean dogs? Well, my big brother used to sell peeks of my naked body for a cup of whiskey until my twelfth birthday, and then he started selling lots more than that for a cup of whiskey or cornmeal or even coins a time or two.

When I turned thirteen years old, I was already getting a mite big around the middle. I did not need rags anymore to clean up the blood that Mama told me I should not talk about, and then Mama figured out I was with child, and she nearly slapped me to death. Caswell laughed and told her I'd been lying down with the traveling preacher, which was surely not the truth.

"Caswell's going to hell, Mama."

"If he goes, you're going with him."

"That's not so, Mama."

Then, of course, she gave me another slap right on my face. I did not know why Mama loved Caswell so much and hated me something awful, but it had always been that way. Even when I tried to tell her what Caswell let boys do to me, she would not listen and would slap me and scream at me for telling lies about

Caswell, who was truly wicked through and through, but she thought he was her most wonderful child.

There really was a traveling preacher, like Caswell said. The preacher rode from town to town across the prairie and wandered here and there, showing up whenever he wanted and leaving whenever he pleased. Some people were always fretting that Sangamon needed a real church and a regular preacher, but somehow nothing ever came of all that talk.

The new preacher had come to Sangamon only two times, and the first time was a freezing cold day, maybe January. He was talking to folks at the general store when I went to fetch headache powders for Mama. Mostly people acted like I was not even there unless I talked up loud, but sometimes folks would get an eye on me and decide I dirtied up the town.

"Git," they'd say. "Git on home now."

And if I did not move right quick, they'd take a step or two closer and look real mean like they were trying to chase away a filthy old dog with a bad sickness.

The first day I saw that preacher, though, he turned to look at me as I came in the door, and he watched me all the time I was telling the grocer, Mr. Jeremiah Frost, what I needed to buy for Mama. I paid the preacher no mind, knowing I did not even have time to warm my bare hands by the potbellied stove, because I had to hurry those powders home or I'd face Mama's screaming and hitting.

The next time I saw the preacher was in the middle of summer. It was a fine day, and I was walking in the woods by the Sangamon River, watching the sunny spots shining through the leaves and dancing on top of the muddy water. The old scruffy dog who lived in the little place with the Indian called Fish was following me down toward the river. We were only a little ways from the road when I pulled up my skirt to my knees and waded into the water and let the black mud squish between my toes.

Then I heard the clopping of a horse moving along the road, and I turned around to see who was coming, knowing I could not count on that dog for any help since he only had one eye and three legs and no matter how brave he acted, there was not anything he could do. I was happy to see it was the preacher, because I thought he was a good man and would not hurt anybody.

The preacher did look right fine sitting up straight and tall on that big spotty horse. He had grown his hair down to his shoulders, and it was as yellow as that stuff hanging off the end of Miz Gray's ears of corn. His eyes were blue and he had a bit of whiskers on his face but not like a real beard. I bent down and pretended to wash the mud off my feet, thinking that if he would go on by, I would not have to say anything, but at the same time wishing he'd stop and talk to me. It got very quiet there in the woods, and after a time I sneaked a look and found the preacher was sitting there on his horse, watching me with a little smile on his face.

"Good day," he said to me.

I looked at him, wondering what he was thinking about, and the funniest feeling came over me, like sunshine and butterflies, and I could tell that preacher knew everything about me, maybe things I did not even know myself.

"You should come to the bible meeting tonight, little sister. Bring your mama and daddy, your brothers and sisters. We'll be in the schoolyard in Sangamon Village."

When the preacher talked, his words were strong and loud like the ringing of the school bell, but at the same time, the sound came floating over me smooth as honey dripping onto a warm sourdough biscuit. I felt like my tongue was stuck to my teeth, and I could not even swallow, so I must have looked stupid standing there with my mouth hanging open. But the preacher just smiled again and waved his hand. Then he poked that big old horse's side with his heel to get it moving.

What he said surely would make people laugh. Bring your mama and daddy and brothers and sisters? I never saw my daddy in all my born days, and I was not even sure Mama knew who my daddy was, because she would not tell me anything about him. Mama would've never gone to a bible meeting, with her having the shame of her own thirteen-year-old child, which was me, being with child. And could you even think on a man as evil as Caswell showing up? All the bibles would smoke and the preacher would fall over in a dead faint.

After I started figuring on how many of the people in Sangamon were doing wicked things they ought not be doing, I wondered if there'd be anyone at that bible meeting. I thought most of the town would be right ashamed to sit before God and the preacher, especially the men that paid Caswell to drag me to the stables in the middle of the night, where they did their business on me and then snuck on home thinking nobody would know. Sometimes, I wondered if God paid even half a mind to the goings-on in Sangamon.

There was other stuff that I learned about because I'd be quiet and mostly people never even saw me. I knew that Miz Wallace, who taught over at the school and was nice as could be and gave me books and helped me learn my numbers and letters, well, she bought a bottle of whiskey from the peddler every month, and she stayed in her little house and got drunk every Saturday. On Mondays she sat at her desk with her head in her hands and made the children sit still and take turns reading real soft, almost whispering.

I also knew that Gabe Swinney, who owned the feed store, wandered around town after dark and peeked in windows. Miz Wallace was so sick and forgetful, what with her drinking and all, that she forgot to pull her curtains closed or turn off her lights when she took off her clothes, and my friend Annie Gray, who had a big farm down the road from town, went in to Miz Wallace's house and took care of the teacher when she felt poorly, even all night long sometimes.

There are lots of things I saw, and those things made me wonder what folks thought of when they went to a prayer meeting and listened to the preacher, knowing they'd been doing secret things that were not right. Of course, maybe they were all like Caswell and did not really give a care for what God or the preacher or anyone else said.

After I'd seen the preacher at the river, I snuck back to town. Caswell was hanging out in front of the feed store, so I ducked into the alley alongside the blacksmith shop so I could watch him. He was leaning against a post, most likely figuring on what no good, mean thing he could do next. And then here came the preacher on his horse, moseying up the street right to where Caswell was standing.

Just as they were as close to Caswell as they could get, they stopped, and the preacher turned his head and looked into Caswell's eyes like he was going to say howdy. But I saw real clear, and the preacher had a frown on his face like he thought something was terrible wrong.

Caswell made a squinty-eyed face with the corners of his mouth turned up like a smile. It was not really a smile, though. Caswell's eyes were downright burning with meanness.

The preacher went on, and Caswell turned around real sudden before I had a chance to jump back, and he gave me that bad look like he gave the preacher, and I ran all the way home, slamming the door and making Mama start screaming at me again, which seemed like all she ever did anyway.

CHAPTER TWO:
WHY MARY PROUD LOVED CASWELL
AND HATED JO MAE

Mary stood by her rumpled bed and stared at the sheets, worn thin from years of use. They needed to be scrubbed and hung out to dry, but it seemed too much of an effort. So she pulled the wool blanket over the sheets and her lumpy goose-down pillow.

Jo Mae ran inside the cabin, slamming the heavy, wooden door so hard Mary felt the floor shudder. She grabbed the pillow from under the blanket and threw it at Jo Mae. The child ducked and ran back outside. Frowning in frustration, Mary smoothed her stringy hair away from her face and tied it back with a strip of cloth she'd cut from a flour sack.

Every time she saw Jo Mae, she thought of Henri de Montagne, the man who had offered Mary and Caswell protection when she was alone and vulnerable, and then had abandoned her the moment he learned she was to have his child. She hated him, and could not help hating Jo Mae as well. The child's belligerence and independence were intolerable. She was impossible to control, insufferably impudent, and now pregnant.

Mary often thought that one more burden, no matter how small, could break her spirit and send her to an early grave. Thank goodness she had Caswell, born of her Philadelphia marriage to her only true love, David Proud. Caswell resembled his father. When Mary looked into his eyes she felt she would swoon at the reminder of her darling David and how violently he had died.

She sat down in her rocking chair, leaned her head against the rocker's wooden headrest, and closed her eyes. Rocking soothed her soul. She moved her foot to set the chair in motion, a slow and gentle tempo accompanied by the rhythmic sweep of her grimy skirt against the wood floor. She adjusted the cadence of her movement to three-four time to mimic the waltz.

Seeing herself as she once had been, young and beautiful, aglow with the certainty all eyes were on her, she thought of the last great party she'd attended many years before. Her gown of pale yellow silk overlaid with sheer white organza had brushed the ballroom floor with every turn. Her dark hair swept into a stylish coil at her crown. Tiny diamonds sparkling in her ears. Her long graceful neck had been bare, her shoulders and arms draped with an organza shawl. When she accepted that first dance with David Proud, she felt the night would never end. In truth, the ball in 1812 was the last time she'd worn a dress as lovely as the yellow silk and danced the night away.

Mary Archer was the only daughter of James and Priscilla, second-generation English immigrants with vague connections to lords and ladies. Mary liked to imagine herself a direct descendant of royalty, but knew in her heart her mother's haughty demeanor was a sham to cover her insecurity. Always concerned about her social standing, Priscilla cultivated friend-ships with the wealthiest and most socially prominent English immigrants. Close friends of the well-to-do Torthwaite family, Priscilla and James conspired with young Adam Torthwaite's parents to bring Adam and nineteen-year-old Mary together. They two had become engaged and planned to marry in the fall.

At the Torthwaite's spring ball, however, Mary made eye contact with a dashing soldier from across the buffet table. She fell in love with David Proud on the spot.

"David," she had cooed after dancing three waltzes in a row with another man, then ignoring her fiancé and returning to David's side. "Could you bring me a cup of punch? I'm quite warm." He did as Mary asked. She rewarded him by entering his name on her dance card.

Later in the evening, Mary approached David again and peeked through her dark eyelashes, giving them a tiny flutter for added effect. "Goodness, I don't know where Adam has wandered off to. David, could you fetch my shawl?" He rushed to do her bidding.

Adam, who huddled in conversation with the elder Torthwaite and Mary's father, seemed to ignore the flirtation. Mary watched her fiancé for a moment, then turned her back and placed her gloved fingers on David's arm.

When the evening was over, with no thought of her engagement to Adam, or that David might not be socially acceptable in Priscilla's eyes, Mary danced about the parlor in their spacious house as she delivered her news to her parents. Priscilla pursed her lips, flared her nostrils, and cried out. Her angular body dropped to the floor with all the grace of a rag doll.

Mary's father, alarmed his wife would awaken from her faint in a rage and make his life miserable for days, knelt by her side and felt for her pulse.

"Mary Louise, if you wed this common soldier, I'll disinherit you at once," her father said as he glowered at his daughter.

"Now, Daddy, you know David is not common. He's quite a good chum of Adam's. Their families are related."

"Related how, Mary?"

Priscilla's eyelashes fluttered and she opened her eyes. As Priscilla struggled to sit up, Mary and her father each took an arm and helped her to her feet.

Mary patted her mother on the shoulder, then waved her hand in the air as though to dismiss her father's question. "Oh,

I don't know. Their mothers are cousins by marriage or some such thing. What does it matter?"

Mary knew her father had little interest in David Proud's pedigree unless the Prouds were more powerful politically and financially than the Torthwaites. Unfortunately, Mary had learned nothing about David's family except his father's occupation—printer. It was unlikely to impress either of her parents. But there was another way in which David might advance the Archers' status in the coming days. She'd heard the men talking, knew of the British attacks on American ships, the kidnapping of American sailors for service to the king in England's war with Napoleon. "If there's to be a war, Daddy—"

"There will indeed war," her father proclaimed. "Pennsylvania will vote aye in the majority, and the rest of the country must do the same. We'll have the British on the run before summer's end."

Mary and her father guided Priscilla to the love seat near the fireplace and fussed over her. Priscilla pulled a handkerchief from her sleeve and dabbed at her eyes.

Mary sighed. Her mother might fake a few tears, but crying was not her way. There would be more discussion of this matter as time went on.

"How can you possibly talk about war at a time like this?" Priscilla said. "Our daughter has done us far more harm than the British will."

Mary's father remained silent, but she knew his thoughts. She'd eavesdropped on many of the discussions he had with others in his study, and she'd heard what else he had on his mind besides war. His plan included public service, and that translated to a run for governor of the State of Pennsylvania.

"Let me remind you, Father, the Archers and the Torthwaites have very strong ties to England. If there is a war, being seen as a British sympathizer could be most destructive, especially during an election campaign. Being the father-in-law of a soldier in the service of our great country, however, a soldier like David Proud . . . well, that would undoubtedly please the voters."

Her father regarded her thoughtfully, but did not comment.

Over the next few days, Mary realized her mother made every effort to sabotage the new romance and force Mary to mend her relationship with Adam. Assuming Priscilla applied constant pressure to her husband behind her daughter's back, Mary did the same whenever she found her father alone.

"Oh, Daddy," she begged, "don't listen to Mother. She doesn't understand. She doesn't care if I'm happy. David has great ambitions, wonderful plans for our future. He's educated, and being a soldier will speak well for him when he's ready to practice law, or perhaps go into politics like you. And besides, I love David."

Mary caught a brief glance of herself in the mirror over the fireplace and quickly raised the back of her hand to her forehead. She stepped closer to the fire, hoping the fumes from the burning pine log would trigger a few tears. Satisfied with the vision she saw from the corner of her eye, she turned a soulful expression toward her father and added a tiny wail to her voice. "I must be with him, no matter what. Mother has forgotten what it's like to be in love."

Mary's father still faced her direction but stared into the distance, apparently distracted by his own thoughts. *What is he thinking about?* she wondered. *My mother?* Or did he mull over his own secret, his desire to run for governor? Mary's mother would faint one more time when she learned of his plans, and she would be incensed if she discovered Mary had known about it for weeks.

"Politics," Priscilla would say. "That's for common people."

If Mary persuaded her father to support her marriage to David, her mother would be furious. But neither she nor her father would suffer long. Her mother always delivered predictions of dire consequences for any action she opposed, then retired to her own room with a box of Belgian chocolates and a book. The household would be at peace until the harridan recovered from her pout and resumed rule over her domain with her pinched expression and harsh rhetoric.

Mary sighed and hoped for the best. According to her mother, Adam could have called David out and challenged him to a duel after that evening. Instead, he ignored David and sent an intermediary to Mary's father to request the return of a family heirloom—the ring he'd given his bride-to-be. David's disloyalty and Mary's unfaithfulness went unpunished.

As the days passed, Mary hoped to regain her mother's co-operation by arranging a large wedding with Philadelphia's most prominent citizens invited. It might have worked if David had not been a soldier. Recently ordered to join the regulars under Captain Nathan Heald at Fort Dearborn in the Illinois Territory, David had to leave Philadelphia immediately.

That Fort Dearborn was a minimally staffed defense post of soldiers and militia, along with a few wives and children, Mary ignored. That hostile Indians roamed the surrounding countryside gave her no pause. Nothing could dissuade Mary from the adventurous life she imagined for herself and her handsome soldier.

She planned to bear his children—two boys for him and at least one girl for her. In addition, she would do everything she could to support her husband's career—climbing to the top of whatever social order ruled the military compound and planning parties and balls attended by dignified men in uniform and ladies in fine gowns. Perhaps even employ a few of those poor pathetic Indians in her service—once the army had tamed them, of course.

Mary focused her attention on David and her plans for their

future. As far as she was concerned, the matter was settled. When her parents suggested she wait a year before marrying, she lifted her chin, refused to answer, and left the room. When her father told her the West was unsettled and dangerous, Mary scoffed.

In June of 1812, two months after first seeing each other across the buffet table, and seven days after President James Madison signed the declaration of war against the British, Mary and David exchanged vows in the garden at her parents' home. Only their families and dearest friends attended. After a brief reception, they climbed aboard the buggy that carried them to the Liberty Inn where their bags and trunks waited.

After only one night alone, David and Mary began the eight-week journey to Fort Dearborn, a voyage that felt like eight years to Mary. Her first letter to her parents was filled with glowing reports of their travels as she attempted to justify her new life to her mother. Soon, however, she began to tell the truth.

July 1, 1812

Dearest Mother and Father,

I cannot begin to describe the appalling conditions of this mode of travel. Although our brief stay on the great steamboat, named the New Orleans, *from Pittsburgh was exciting and most comfortable, we had to disembark and continue our travels by other means, as the New Orleans travels down the Mississippi to the port city of the same name. Alas, we were to go in a northerly direction. The boats on which we travel now are infested with intolerable numbers of vermin that swarm onto the berths at night and do not allow one the tiniest bit of sleep. The river smells of rotted fish, and the mattresses reek of mildew and men who never bathe. I cannot sleep unless I have a lavender sachet pressed to my nose. Dirt and debris are overlooked, even if a refined lady or gentleman has booked passage . . .*

July 16, 1812

Dearest Mother,

Yesterday the strangest band of men and women came on board the Kelly O'Dair, *which is what our boat is named. They wore the rough clothes of the backwoodsmen we've seen before, but we soon realized some of the wretched folk were women. In trousers, Mother. They seemed very strong, wore their hair cut short, and conversed, drank, and worked as did the men. I've seen nothing like it before. I immediately left their presence and stayed by David's side until these unladylike creatures disembarked . . .*

September 4, 1812

Dearest Daddy,

I've addressed this letter to you because its contents might shock poor Mother. It's best if you break this news to her more gently than I tell it here. I can hardly write of what has happened, and pray you have not heard of these events, which would horrify you and keep you and Mother in an agony of worry concerning our safety. But it must be told. Less than three weeks before we arrived at Fort Dearborn, the British captured Fort Mackinac in the Michigan Territory. Hearing this, and fearing a British incursion south to Fort Dearborn, Captain Heald abandoned the fort with his soldiers, militia, and the women and children. With an escort of Indians, Captain Heald hoped to make his way safely to Fort Wayne in Indiana.*

Instead, and this is the frightening part, Daddy, hostile Indians attacked and killed many, including women and children. Others escaped, only to end up in the hands of the British.

We are thankful we had not yet arrived at Fort Dearborn, but most fearful that such devastating savagery will be repeated . . .

Two months later Mary received a communication in return. Her father had been dissuaded from running for office after another potential candidate aimed an accusing finger, declaring James a British spy who expected to govern Pennsylvania after England won the war. Mary concluded her father had feared for his life and the safety of his wife and his property. He apparently gave little thought to the plight of his daughter. She received a brief note from him, telling her of his own perilous situation. He added that Mary's mother had taken to her bed in shock.

Mary assumed her mother had feigned illness to avoid her friends and others whose high opinion she valued, so Mary did not take the information seriously. She assumed her father had relayed the story of the massacre, and Mary was hurt that her mother ignored her daughter's tale of horror. Even so, Mary continued her letters, always adding a note that she hoped her mother's health soon improved and that the silly nonsense about her father being a British spy had been resolved.

Mary received no more letters from her parents.

During the next two years, Mary and David lived in a series of small, primitive camps in the Illinois Territory from the Fort Dearborn area to Galena. Mary was grateful she did not become pregnant right away. Her dream of fancy balls and elegant dining became a sad memory. Now that she knew what her life would be like for several more years, she realized how inconvenient and dangerous pregnancy and childbirth would be.

Two years after their arrival in the territory, however, Mary delivered her first baby, a tiny replica of David Proud. She could tell from her husband's expression that this was the greatest moment of his life, and for that she was grateful. A Methodist minister, who served seven military locations in the region, christened the baby Caswell James Proud in June of 1814.

Illinois had not yet attained statehood, and small bands of

hostile Indians still wandered their homeland, burning homes, killing livestock, and murdering the invaders. One July day, only one month after the birth of his son, Lieutenant David Proud and his patrol surprised the renegades in the act of raiding a settlement just outside the fort. The Indians fought back, killing two soldiers before the entire band of savages was slaughtered.

David was one of the two soldiers who died in the battle.

A few hours later, Mary, carrying Caswell in her arms, stood with another woman near the wagons and waited while the soldiers recovered their dead. Mary asked if she might keep her husband's pistols and sabre, but was refused. Good weapons were in short supply due to increased demand on the eastern shores as the British moved toward the capital in Washington.

As her wagon joined the caravan to carry the two bodies through the gates of the fort, the women observed the field still strewn with dead horses and a dozen lifeless savages.

If not for the babe in her arms, Mary would have plunged a knife into her own heart so she could be buried beside her beloved David. Instead, she trembled as she hugged Caswell close to her breast and turned away from the bodies littering the field.

Chapter Three:
Gray Fish of the Kickapoo

On a summer day in the White Man's year 1814, Gray Fish and the other Kickapoo elders strode resolutely toward the battleground to gather their dead. The old men led horses that dragged stretchers attached to long poles. Behind the horses came the women, young and old, keening and chanting—an eerie sound that drifted through the air like the haunting wail of the blue coat's horn.

Among the fallen was fifty-three-year-old Gray Fish's only child, Running Wolf, a rebellious young warrior who had ignored his father's counsel and participated in the raid.

In spite of the teachings of Kenekuk, the Kickapoo prophet, and in spite of his father's warning, Running Wolf did not listen. He had rejected the goals of tribal elders who wished to make peace with the White Man. The younger warriors ridiculed the old ones and their foolish hopes. They argued that Indian tribes could not peacefully retain control of their own lands in the face of the settlers who swarmed across the prairies like clouds of locusts.

When Running Wolf rode away with his band of raiders, he did not look back.

Now Gray Fish came to take his son's body home and to say the ceremonial words that would send Running Wolf's spirit to a place of serenity.

Grief hung in the air over the battleground—grief as heavy as three tightly woven blankets draped over a man's shoulders.

Gray Fish stopped at the top of the hill. The blue coats and the women were hauling their dead away in buckboards. One woman caught his attention. The one carrying a baby. Gray Fish stared at her curiously. Her white face showed no emotion. *Does she not mourn?* he wondered. *Does she not hate?* Kickapoo women expressed their feelings with much noise and passion. Gray Fish had assumed all women behaved this way.

Despite their open demonstrations of grief, the females of his tribe were strong of body and mighty of spirit—this he knew. *The frail, young white woman must be weak,* Gray Fish thought. And afraid. He watched until she turned away.

The night after the battle, Gray Fish walked with his son in a dream and listened with great sorrow as the young man boasted of his own courage in battle. As long as Gray Fish lived, and until father and son were joined in the realm of the Great Spirit, Gray Fish knew he would continue to mourn his son's useless sacrifice.

After the death of Running Wolf, and with the persistent rebellion of tribes in the Illinois and Michigan territories, Gray Fish foresaw continued violence with no hope of a successful conclusion for his people. He wanted no part of the killing. However, his pride would not let him meekly submit to the White Man's will.

During the summer of 1818, Gray Fish became so alarmed by the increasing power and control of Black Hawk, a Sauk warrior with great influence over certain Kickapoo bands, that Gray Fish and his wife left the Kickapoo tribe behind. They traveled south, away from the threat of war, but Gray Fish's wife died shortly after their journey began. Gray Fish spent the next two years alone, wandering, working from time to time as a guide.

Finally, in 1820, Gray Fish claimed his own piece of land near the river that bordered the Village of Sangamon. He built a large *wikiyapi* from branches, reeds, and weeping willow whips and furnished the inside of his house with animal pelts, rocks, and the blankets he'd kept from his years with the tribe. He cleared brush and rocks from a small area so he could plant corn, squash, and beans. Gradually he made his presence known to the townsfolk, easing his way into their lives as a trader of meat, fish, and furs.

Gray Fish was tolerated, even kindly by some, but he never forgot he was an Indian, viewed as less than those who were white. That would not change, he thought, at least not in his lifetime.

Eighteen years after the battle in which Running Wolf died, and less than a month after soldiers captured Black Hawk and the bloody Sauk war ended, the federal government convinced most of the Kickapoo to move west of the Mississippi River. A few stubborn members of the tribe were still scattered throughout Illinois. Knowing the soldiers would forcibly remove them from their homes, the Indians stayed out of sight and out of trouble, doing nothing that would attract attention. Gray Fish was one of those Indians.

Across Indiana and Illinois, men seeking to establish trading posts, gristmills, and other businesses followed the settlers who had established farms and ranches throughout the prairie. By 1832, the Village of Sangamon contained a general store, a feed store, a saloon, a school, a doctor, and a blacksmith shop attached to a stable large enough to board three horses.

Once a month, the seventy-one-year-old Gray Fish left his home by the river and hauled furs, game birds, fish, or deer meat to the general store to trade for coffee, salt, cornmeal, flour, and tobacco. He used a sled he'd constructed from willow branches and a gray, tattered canvas recovered from the ruins of a Conestoga wagon, long ago abandoned upriver. Gray Fish dragged his goods by hand since he did not have a horse.

"Hey, Fish, what do you have for me today?" Jeremiah Frost, owner of the general store, paused in the doorway and leaned on the broom he used to sweep dried mud from the steps in front of his building.

Few people in the village bothered to learn the Indian's name or any words of the Kickapoo language. The Indian called himself Fish and so did anyone else who wanted to treat him with respect. Fish was certain most of the villagers could not identify him as Kickapoo, even though most were aware of the tribe's violent history and might consider Fish a danger to the community if they had made the connection.

Fish pulled his load into the store and folded the cloth back to reveal his barter. Two of the men who'd been sitting on the porch in front of the store followed the Indian inside and peered over his shoulder.

"I'd take the pheasant," said one.

"That's a nice one," said the other. "What say we each take half? Depending on Jeremiah's price, of course. What else you got, Fish?"

Peeling back the leaves with which he'd wrapped two small carp, a large bass, and two venison steaks, Fish grunted and waited for Jeremiah to calculate what profit he might make off the Indian's goods, and how much he could afford to trade from his supplies, especially costly items like salt and tobacco. Until the storekeeper made an acceptable offer, Fish stood silently, using a nearly imperceptible shake of his head to decline a price. With the same impassive expression, he grunted once when the trade met with his approval. He loaded his bartered goods on his sled and pulled it out the door.

"You, Injun, get out of my way!"

The hairs rose on the back of Fish's neck. He clenched his jaw. Maintaining a steady pace, refusing to cringe or back away,

Fish tried to push past Caswell Proud and pull his supplies down the two wooden steps to the dusty road that ran in front of the store.

"Hellfire, you red bastard, I said to get out of my way."

"Ah, leave him alone, Caswell," said Jeremiah, who had returned to the doorway when he heard Caswell's voice. "He ain't doing no harm."

"The hell he ain't," Caswell mocked. "That stuff you gave him is food out of the mouths of us town folks."

"I didn't give it to him. I traded him for it. Why don't you come in here and see what he brought?"

"Oh, hellfire, like you thought Mama and me could afford fresh meat?" Caswell followed Jeremiah into the store as the men who'd negotiated for the pheasant slipped out and headed down the road, apparently more interested in avoiding Caswell than in securing more of the game.

Curious, Fish dropped the rope he used to pull his load and followed the two men back inside the store.

"There's a couple of carp here," Jeremiah said.

"Mama don't eat mud feeders. I got something I can trade for that other fish, though." The eighteen-year-old leaned forward and leered. Jeremiah blushed and stammered while he looked around as if to make sure they were alone.

Fish stood still, feeling invisible, as the grocer bustled past him and peeked out the door. After he'd checked in all directions, Jeremiah returned inside, wrapped the bass back in its leafy covering, and secured it with a piece of string.

"What time?" Jeremiah asked as he handed over Caswell's purchase.

"Ten o'clock," Caswell answered.

"Don't let her start hollering this time."

"She won't. I told her I'd beat her black and blue if she ever did that again."

Caswell walked toward the door, gave Fish a shove as he went by, then laughed as Fish stumbled against a barrel and fell to his knees.

Fish scrambled to his feet and hurried outside, fearing Caswell might steal his supplies. He sighed in relief when he saw Caswell trotting along the road toward the broken-down cabin where he lived with his mother and sister.

"Hey, Fish. Everything okay?" Jeremiah stepped outside and watched as the Indian grabbed up the rope of his sled.

"Good. All good," Fish answered. He turned away, looped the rope across his shoulder to distribute the weight, and pulled the sled down the main road toward the river.

He was puzzled. Occasionally the men of the town acknowledged his presence and treated him like any other man. Most of the time, however, they ignored him, especially the women, as though he wore a medicine man's cloak that let him travel in the world of ghosts and spirits while still viewing those in the earthbound world of humans and animals.

Caswell Proud, the one man in Sangamon Fish hated and feared the most, might acknowledge, disdain, ignore, or threaten. In the past, Caswell had not struck Fish. After the shove in the store, it was only a matter of time. He must always be prepared.

Fish shook his head and wondered again, like he had so many times over the years, what white folks were made of, what they thought about right and wrong, and why the Great Spirit had let them come and change the Indian way.

He wondered why he stayed here, to live among these odd people with their peculiar customs, instead of traveling across the great river to live among his own people. He must think more about leaving this place before he became too old to travel such a great distance.

And finally, he thought about Caswell.

An evil spirit had found its way into the mother's womb, Fish decided. Perhaps the white woman did not know how to ward off evil before bearing her child. Too bad.

CHAPTER FOUR:
CASWELL THE PROVIDER

Pleased with himself, Caswell plopped the wrapped fish on the table and waited for Mama to say something nice.

She leaned forward in her rocker. "What is it?"

"Come and see." He untied the string and peeled the leaves off the black bass.

"Oh, my," she said. She stood by the table, staring as though she'd never seen a fish before.

Caswell knew how she felt. They'd eaten no meat for a week, except bits of beef jerky thrown in a pot of water with the vegetables from Miz Gray, the rich farming lady who gave them food from her garden. Caswell didn't like her much. Maybe because he knew she didn't like him. She was downright sickening with all that sweet talk, looking down her nose while letting everybody know she was out doing her Christian duty.

There were a few of Miz Gray's summer vegetables left in the bin by the stove. Mama would cook them together with the fish in the only kettle they owned. She would save the largest helping for him, dividing the rest between herself and Jo Mae.

"Where did you get it?" Mama asked, never taking her gaze away from the bass.

"That old Injun," answered Caswell. "I helped him bring his load into town and he paid me in trade."

"I guess he's good for something then. Where's Jo Mae?"

"Don't know. Haven't seen her."

"Find her and send her out to Miss Gray's house. See what else we can get for the pot."

When Caswell was six years old, Mama spent one long night screaming at the top of her lungs and shouting at Miz Gray, who ran back and forth from the fireplace to the bed with towels and hot water. Miz Gray told him over and over again Mama would be fine soon and he should try to sleep, but he didn't believe her. Caswell hid under the covers of his bed with his hands over his ears and his eyes tightly closed, sure he had driven Mama plumb crazy, as she'd often said he would do.

If he'd known going crazy sounded like that, Caswell might have tried harder to behave the way Mama wanted. Sometimes her wants got him all mixed up. The things that made her mad were also the things that made her pay attention to him. One minute she yelled at him and pushed him away, and then in the next minute she'd run her fingers through his hair and hug him close.

"Caswell, is that blood all over your shirt?" she'd asked earlier, the day before she started all the screeching. Mama had reached for his hands. The skin of her face turned white and her voice had stretched thin and trailed into a whisper. "Are you hurt?"

Caswell had stuck his hands behind his back and examined his shirt. He stared at the floor while he figured out whether he'd done something Mama would call a bad thing.

Trapping that ugly dog? he wondered. Dirty old thing didn't belong to anybody except the Injun that lived by the river. Dog dug in garbage. Killed one of Miz Gray's laying hens. Somebody should have gone out there and shot that dog long before now.

He couldn't figure out why nobody had. All Caswell did was leave a broken egg in the Indian's muskrat trap so the old dog would go after it. He hadn't figured on the dog chewing its own leg off to get free. It disgusted him, nearly made him puke, but he couldn't stop watching while the dog chewed clear through his skin and bones and everything. Before the dog limped away on its three good legs, dragging the chewed up fourth leg still dripping blood, it stared at Caswell for a long time. When it finally went on, it left its paw and a bit of its leg behind.

That's when Caswell had gotten covered with blood. He'd grabbed up that piece of dog, peeled back the skin, and poked at all the bones and the soft parts that felt like meat on a chicken leg.

When Mama had finished checking him over, she asked again where the blood came from.

"Dog got caught in a trap down by the river. I set him free, but he was hurt bad."

"Caswell! You could have been killed. An injured animal can be very dangerous." Since none of the blood was Caswell's, she had yelled at him for scaring her and making a mess. Caswell bowed his head again and tried hard to look sorry. He waited for Mama to stop yelling, and then he promised to always be good ever after. She'd dragged him out to the rain barrel and scooped out enough water to wash most of the blood off his hands.

"Stay out of trouble now," she had said. "I'm tired of hearing complaints from half the town about my child running wild."

"I will, Mama. I will." Caswell patted his pocket. He'd hide the dog's foot before Mama found it and made him throw it away.

The next day he was sitting on a rock in front of the cabin when Mama called him. He stayed put, poking at a beetle with a stick to scare it good before he squished it under his boot. Mama kept on hollering, louder and louder. When the calling began to sound more like screaming, Caswell went inside.

Mama sat on the side of her bed, all bent over and clutching at her belly. Sweat covered her scrunched-up face. She acted like she had a bad case of colic.

"Get Miss Annie Gray," Mama yelled. "Go get her now."

Later, even when Miz Gray patted Mama and talked soft, the screaming went on and on for what seemed like the whole day. Caswell's hands shook as he brought them up to cover his ears. Something was going on he didn't understand. Mama had never acted like this before. It wasn't ever going to stop; even Miz Gray couldn't make it stop.

Maybe Mama had some kind of screaming sickness. Maybe she was going to die. If he didn't have Mama, who would take care of him? Wouldn't be Miz Gray, he figured. Hardly anyone in the town would want him, for that matter.

It was sure the teacher didn't like him. When Mama made him go to school, the teacher didn't pay any attention to him at all unless somebody yelled or cried, and then she'd blame him first like he was the only one who ever did a bad thing.

The girls were scared of him because he'd sneak up behind them and then yell real loud. He scared the boys, too. He told them Injuns would come and scalp them and scalp their mama and daddy and eat the babies, if they had any.

Mostly he didn't go to school. No one cared about that much; at least they didn't say. Mama shrugged her shoulders and taught him his numbers and letters at home, using old pages of *The Sangamon Valley Gazette* that often came wrapped around food or supplies from the general store.

When Mama had finally grown quiet after hours of wailing and carrying on, Miz Gray came out of the bedroom with a bundle of rags in her arms. Caswell threw back his blanket and sat up.

"Your mother's sleeping now," Miz Gray had told him. "You can go talk to her when she wakes up."

"She's not dead?"

"No, child," Miz Gray had answered with a chuckle. "She's not dead. What made you think that?"

"I don't know. Is she crazy?"

"Oh, goodness, no. Here, look at this baby sister of yours. This is what the hollering was all about." Miz Gray crossed the room and sat down on the edge of the bed, held the bundle in her lap, and uncovered a tiny, wrinkled face in a squished-up head. She turned the face toward Caswell so he could see.

"This is your little sister," Miz Gray said.

Caswell stared and pulled back. He'd never seen anything so ugly before, even in a nightmare. The thing was all mixed-up colors—pink, blue, and gray. Its wrinkly skin reminded him of dried-apple faces on the granny dolls he'd seen at the general store.

"What is it?" he whispered.

"It's a baby," Miz Gray said. "Haven't you ever seen a baby before?"

"None that looked like that. Take it away."

Caswell pinched his lips together, wrinkled his nose, and focused on the wall behind the bed. His fingers scratched at the blanket, ready to pull it over his head. Miz Gray held the baby close to her shoulder so Caswell couldn't see its face.

Later, Caswell stood by Mama's bedside and stared at her as she slept. When he saw she was breathing, he dashed by Miz Gray and ran outside. He didn't want to return until Miz Gray took the disgusting monster and went away. His legs had dangled from both sides of the limb on his favorite climbing tree as he watched his own cabin and most of the comings and goings on the main road through the Village of Sangamon. And he waited.

He would have stayed in the tree through the day and even into the night, if he hadn't seen the Injun coming into the village from the river road. The old man stopped at the feed store and lifted his head like an animal sniffing the wind. He had turned slowly toward Caswell's climbing tree and stared so hard it scared Caswell nearly to death. The hairs on the top of his head rose and the back of his neck felt like bugs were crawling on his skin.

Stealing from the Injun's muskrat trap was enough to bring the Injun to town. Maybe hurting the dog made the Injun even madder, worse than messing with the traps. Caswell thought of the scalping stories he'd told other children, then put his hands up to cover his head. His body wobbled on the branch and he almost lost his balance.

The foul-smelling dog's paw in his pocket didn't seem like such a good idea anymore. Caswell grabbed at a branch to steady himself, then scooted backwards to a place where he could hang from a limb and drop to the ground. Saving his scalp was the only thing left on his mind.

Chapter Five:
The Good Woman Annie Gray

Annie Gray stumbled and almost dropped Mary's newborn daughter, Jo Mae, when Caswell shrieked as he dashed in the door. The boy scrambled onto the bed, next to his mother, and stared wide-eyed at the doorway as he clutched the hair on the top of his head.

Mary woke up briefly, turned her back to Caswell, and pulled the comforter over her head.

Annie lowered the baby into the quilt-lined kindling box she had prepared earlier, and rushed to check Caswell for injuries. A foul odor emanated from the boy every time he moved. Annie stepped back a moment, then approached the bed and gently pried the child's grubby hands away from his head. There were no fresh wounds she could see, only dried blood and mud caking his tattered shirt and pants. No bumps or bruises showed through the layers of grime that covered his exposed skin.

Annie released Caswell, who now moaned and sobbed as he struggled to see around her. She turned toward the door to see what had his attention. No one was there.

A thin wail of protest erupted from the wood box. Abruptly, Caswell stopped crying. Annie took one more peek at Caswell, convinced he'd had a fright but not an accident. He stared at the box as though it contained something putrid.

"It's that ugly thing, isn't it? That baby. You take it out of here! It's making an awful noise."

Annie raised her eyebrows as she thought of the commotion

Caswell had made only moments before.

A scuffling sound at the front of the cabin attracted her attention. The Indian, Fish, stood outside the doorway, staring into the room as though waiting to be invited inside. Caswell let out a yelp and tried to hide behind his mother.

So, Annie thought, *Caswell got himself into trouble with the Indian.*

"Fish," she said. "What's wrong?"

He acknowledged Annie's question with a nod, but did not answer, clearly distracted by the noise coming from the dark corner of the room. Annie walked to the wood box and picked up the baby. Shushing and humming as she rocked the tiny bundle back and forth, she pulled the cover away from its face so Fish could see. "It's a girl," she told him.

"Mmm," Fish said. He turned his attention to the bed and the sick, exhausted woman who lay there sleeping.

Annie carried the now-quiet baby back to its makeshift crib, then returned to the doorway where Fish still lingered.

"She will die?" Fish asked.

"No, I think not. But she's very ill."

"Who will take this boy while his mother is sick?" Fish pointed at the quivering child who lay burrowed against Mary's back.

"Take him? Away, you mean? Why, no one, Fish. The boy lives here."

"Who will take care of him? He has a father?"

"Oh, I see. Who will take care of him? No, Caswell's father has been dead a long time. And the baby's father is gone, too. Back to the mountains. I'll do what needs to be done for now. His mother should be better in a few days."

"Mmm. Boy has a name?"

"Caswell."

"Caswell. What does that name mean?"

44

"I'm not sure it means anything."

"Boy needs a different name."

Caswell stopped whining and lay very still.

Must have convinced himself he can't be seen, Annie thought. What had Caswell done? How had he angered the Indian? She trusted Fish under normal circumstances, but had no idea how he might react if Caswell had stolen or damaged his property.

Fish raised his voice so he could be heard across the room. "You. Boy. Caswell. You hear me? You listen now. What you did to old dog was very bad. You stay away from the river. You come back, and old dog and old Indian will send the snake or wolf. Maybe send an evil spirit. Spirit will eat your eyes and make worms crawl in your mouth."

Annie gasped, shocked by the image he'd created for the small boy who now shook in obvious terror as he curled closer to his mother's unresponsive form. Annie had never heard the Indian speak more than a couple of words at a time, so she had no idea he knew so much English. She wondered what the child had done to elicit such a graphic admonishment from the normally placid old man.

Fish glanced toward Mary's bed. "I know much of this woman. Little girl with this woman and this boy . . . mmm." Fish shook his head and sighed. "Girl needs many good friends. Friends will keep the girl strong. You tell her."

Abruptly Fish turned and strode out the cabin door.

Annie stared after him, wondering if she should have asked more questions about Caswell and what he'd done to the dog. Then she shrugged. Best not to know any more about this family than she already knew.

In the late 1700s, Annie Gray's parents had been among the first English immigrants to move west from Philadelphia into the Illinois Territory, as well as among the first to suffer the loss of their home and animals to a marauding band of Indians. They'd carried on, went into debt, rebuilt, and then saw their buildings shaken to rubble during the three winter earthquakes of 1811 and 1812. Again they persevered, working harder than ever. In spite of the bad luck they suffered, the Grays never lost heart, never became bitter or resentful. They extended their charity to all, including runaway slaves who occasionally made their way into the territory.

When the older Grays died fighting a prairie fire in 1815, both having lived into their sixties, they left twenty-five-year-old Annie, their only child, one hundred and sixty acres of fertile land, all the tools to make a good living, and a solid three-room log cabin with two outbuildings. A split-rail fence surrounded an orchard containing eighteen mature fruit trees, most of them apple. A mule, two pigs, and a large flock of chickens contributed to Annie's wealth and to the well-being of her community. And her Guernsey cow. Even though Annie had to walk it ten miles each spring to visit the Castleton's bull, her cow provided revenue from milk sales and the sale of its calves.

The farm sat at the southeast edge of the village, angled toward the river, which curved around the western and southern edges of Sangamon. The river had flooded only twice in the last twenty-five years, but each flood had deposited another layer of thick black muck that made Annie's fields produce beans, corn, and apples that were the best barter crops within fifty miles.

But it was Annie's chickens that first brought Fish to her door. She had greeted the Indian, then nervously waited until he told her what he wanted.

"Trade," he'd finally said. "Want one chicken. Keep for eggs."

"What do you have that you can trade for one laying hen?"

Fish pulled a small bundle off his sled and laid it on the ground. He motioned for Annie to examine the package.

She stepped forward and bent down, peeling the flap back to

see the contents. "Ohh," she breathed. "Really? I may have both of them for one chicken?" Annie pulled two cock pheasants from the tote, dangling them by the legs, admiring the long tail feathers. She laid the dead birds on her front stoop and hurried off to fulfill her part of the bargain.

Before the Indian left with the struggling hen tucked under his arm, he pointed to his own chest and said, "Fish." He waited expectantly until she finally pointed to herself and told him, "My name is Annie." The next time he came to trade, and until Annie finally corrected him, Fish addressed her as "MynameisAnnie."

On the day the Indian threatened Caswell, the day Mary gave birth to Jo Mae, Annie wondered what she should tell Mary. Caswell still cowered on the bed near his mother. What could he have done to Fish's dog? Was his behavior changing from mischievous to malicious?

She had to tell Mary as soon as the woman was strong enough to deal with her difficult son. And what of this new baby? How would *she* survive a lazy mother and a brother who might be showing signs of cruelty?

Was it fair to leave a tiny, helpless soul like Jo Mae in the hands of the Prouds? Would it be better to steal her away in the night? Take her to another town? Find her a new family? Tell Mary Proud the baby had died?

Annie shook her head. She could never steal a child. That would take control out of God's hands. If it were God's will this little girl be born into such a family, then Annie could only pay attention to the Indian's words. She could be a friend to Jo Mae, watch over her, be kind.

With that decision made, Annie gently woke Mary. "I'm leaving for now," Annie said. "To gather up food for supper. The baby's sleeping, over there in the wood box. It'll be time for you to nurse her when I return."

"Where's Caswell?" Mary whispered.

"There on the bed, next to you."

"Is that what smells?" Mary wrinkled her nose in disgust and pulled away from the boy. "Get off the bed, Caswell. Go on, get off!"

Annie gathered her shawl and bonnet and swept out the door as she thought of what she'd bring to Mary's cabin. The washtub, for one thing. She could use it to carry food and cleaning supplies. She already knew Mary had no soap in the cabin—no scrub brush, either. But getting this family fed was the first priority.

As she hurried away, Annie heard Mary call out to Caswell.

"Bring my hairbrush," the woman ordered.

"Lordy," Annie muttered. "Her hairbrush, of all things."

Then she pressed her lips together and chastised herself. It wasn't her place to judge. Annie put her hand up to her own straight brown hair she'd coiled and pinned on top of her head, reminding herself she possessed a bit of vanity as well.

She'd long ago stopped thinking of herself as pretty. After all, she was over thirty, a spinster. But her hair . . . her father had always said her hair was "soft as a butterfly's wing." He said she could be a princess with hair so fine.

One hundred strokes with a brush every night before bed. Annie had performed that ritual as long as she could remember. At least that was one thing she could understand about Mary.

CHAPTER SIX:
MARY PROUD ON HER OWN

Mary took the hairbrush from Caswell, but instead of using it to smooth the tangles in her hair, she turned it over and stroked the once beautiful silver back. Black tarnish had eaten its way into the swirls and intricate flowers etched in the soft metal. The brush and a matching mirror had been a gift from her parents when she was still in school, before she met David and foolishly allowed him to sweep her off her feet and bring her to this harsh, uncivilized country. Mary's eyes grew moist.

The hand mirror that matched the brush was long gone, broken and discarded during the trip to the Illinois Territory. The brush was the only precious thing she had left. Most of her finery—her ball gowns, jewelry, and exquisite shoes—had been sold as she tried to survive after David died.

Tears welled up in Mary's eyes as she thought of her handsome soldier, buried so long ago. She remembered how desperately she had appealed to her father and mother for help. Their house in Philadelphia was her safe haven. All her problems would have been solved if she could have gone home.

Mary had written to her father the day after she buried David.

Daddy,

David is dead. I'm alone in this terrible place, living in a tent. No one is coming to rebuild Fort Dearborn. The army refuses to take us east. They are concerned with controlling the

Indians and pushing them west. They do not have time for us. If you leave us here, we'll die. I know we will.

She wrote again the next day.

Mother, my heart is broken. I cannot eat a thing. My milk has dried up. I cannot tend to Caswell. I'm afraid he will starve. Please send Daddy. I cannot make the trip back to Philadelphia without help.

Months passed before she understood why there had been no answer to the countless letters filled with anguish she had sent to Philadelphia by any means available.

Young Adam Torthwaite, the fiancé Mary had jilted when she fell in love with David, stood stiffly in the doorway of the women's tent near the old Fort Dearborn site. He cleared his throat and ran his finger around his collar as though it had grown uncomfortably tight.

Mary sat on the edge of her narrow bed, her shoulders slumped and her mouth sagging open in amazement. She could not believe what he'd told her. She stared at him in dismay. If she believed Adam's tale, his own life and fortune had changed as drastically as hers. And Mary's parents had fallen victim to even more serious events. Mary knew her father, James, had abandoned his plans to run for governor after his enemies accused him of being a British spy. Now she learned he had sold their house and furnishings before his arrest on charges of treason. Her mother had died soon after. Adam reported Priscilla was rumored to have taken her own life, but he could not verify whether the story was true or false. Officially, she suffered a heart attack.

There was no refuge in Philadelphia for Mary after all. She felt dizzy and put her hand to her head. Her forehead felt clammy and the palms of her hands damp. She shivered.

"With the British marching toward Washington, and Madison preparing to remove the government to Virginia, the eastern seaboard is nearly as unsettled and dangerous as these territories," Adam added.

"What will happen to my father?" Mary tugged at the tangled strands of hair that hung around her face and tucked them behind her ears.

"Officials are preoccupied, preparing for war. But there will eventually be a trial."

"Will he go to prison?"

Adam looked away, mumbling something Mary could not believe she'd heard correctly.

"What did you say? Did you say he could be hanged?"

"I'm sorry, Mary. There was little we could do."

"Did your father step forward, defend our family?"

"My father and mother have gone to England."

Mary jumped to her feet and took a defiant step in Adam's direction. "Your parents ran away? While mine, who were innocent, have lost everything?"

"Yes."

"Yet you are here."

"I am. Your father asked me to come."

"Ah. And what message do you bring?"

"I am to deliver his love." Adam's voice cracked, but he quickly recovered. "And his deepest regret he cannot come himself."

"No more? It was hardly worth the long trip."

Adam shuffled his feet. "The trip was indeed long, a hardship, Mary, both in cost and in time . . . but I wanted to see you again." He put his hand to his mouth and coughed. When he spoke again, his voice was strong and his tone firm. "I am leaving at once."

"Could I not return to Philadelphia with you?"

"Not for Philadelphia, Mary. I'm going to Fort Detroit."

"But the British hold Detroit!"

"Yes."

Mary's knees gave way, and she dropped down to sit on the edge of her cot. If she had married Adam instead of David, she would have married a traitor. She could not believe it. And David—David would have been appalled. What should she do? Where would she go? Mary left the words unspoken, unwilling to show weakness before this man to whom she'd once been betrothed.

"I may as well say it, Mary. You and your baby must remain here. You must find a way to survive. Your father said you were—"

"My father! Does he know about you?"

"Yes, I told him when I went to see him, after his arrest. I knew about your letters and thought I might be able to help."

"Help? What help do you have to offer?"

"Your father said you're skilled with a needle. Could you perhaps become a dressmaker?"

Her chin came up and she felt her eyes grow wide. "Me? You want me to be a dressmaker?"

"You're well-educated," he hastened to add. "You've studied French and literature. You could teach school."

Mary's astonishment turned to shock. She saw Adam shift nervously and check his pocket watch.

"Mary, these are difficult times. We do what we have to do." He shrugged. "Besides, you'll marry again. I'm sure there are many fine young men here in Illinois who—"

She shook her head to silence him. The thought of marrying one of the filthy ruffians she saw every day made her sick. But she sensed the finality in Adam's voice and for the first time felt a shiver of apprehension. She'd always been able to get whatever she wanted from her father. Now her father could not help her and might even die. Everything had gone wrong, and she didn't know what to do about it.

"I gave you advice, Mary. Take it. Here." He thrust an envelope at her. "Your father sold the things you left in your room. He sent you the proceeds."

Mary stood and reached out for the envelope in his hand. "My canopy bed?"

"Sold."

"My grandmother's jewelry? That was to be mine."

"Sold."

"I guess you must be going, then," she said. She clutched the envelope in both hands and waited, her back straight. She hoped her expression showed no emotion.

Adam braved her rigid stance to take one of her hands, pull it gently toward him, and kiss her fingers.

Mary pulled her hand back. As Adam walked away, she lifted her arm as though she intended to call out to him. But she said nothing and let her hand drop to her side.

Once Adam departed, Mary collapsed onto the cot and closed her eyes. Too shocked even to cry, she let his words flow back into the room and swirl around her head. She thrust the envelope of cash into the bodice of her dress. Little good that would do her in a world that dealt mostly in barter. She would hide it away, spend it only for Caswell. But, work! What kind of work?

The only needlework Mary had ever done was the decorative embroidery edging her fine linens. As for teaching, there were more people capable of educating children than there were schools in this godforsaken land. Anyway, she had never liked children much. Already she dreaded the day tiny Caswell, with his father's blue eyes and sandy hair, would come under the influence of rowdy, snot-nosed creatures like the ones who ran roughshod through the camp.

Having shrugged aside Adam's suggestions, Mary realized she needed a plan. She considered the army officers she'd met over the last two years and the businessmen who flocked to the lead mining region over near Galena. Finding a man with money and prestige who wasn't already married would prove to be a challenge, she thought, unless she settled for a liaison outside of marriage. Perhaps, she mused, if the rewards were adequate. She was a lady. She would do whatever necessary to avoid working as a common tradesperson.

Caswell whimpered, drawing Mary's attention. Adam hadn't even glanced Caswell's way. Everything Adam had told her rushed back and washed over her. For a moment she could not breathe. Caswell's whimper became an impatient wail. Mary struggled to her feet, picked up her son, and walked back and forth by her cot, weeping quietly against the soft skin at the side of Caswell's neck.

Mary chose to entertain men to support herself and her son.

Even though David had been killed in the line of duty, Mary could no longer keep quarters inside the military compound. There were not enough buildings or supplies for the government to provide room and board for all the soldiers' widows and orphans, so Mary found a tiny cabin on the outskirts of a trading and shipping settlement on the great lake. There she kept watch for those men who appeared to be of substantial means. Always playing the lady, she persuaded them to trade with her.

Once the war with the British ended early in 1815, the Americans again turned their attention to westward expansion. The reconstruction of Fort Dearborn was completed in 1816. Mary then latched onto a high-ranking officer assigned to the newly rebuilt fort. Her kind and generous lover rarely came to visit, but when he did, he brought food, the latest bonnets or delicate undergarments from the East, and even a heavy cloak made of wool.

There were military demands on his time, of course, but he also had a shrewd and attentive wife to keep him occupied. His stolen moments with Mary were few.

Her problems began in earnest later that year when the captain was promoted to major and ordered to move his troops west of the Mississippi River to supervise the movement of Indian tribes that had agreed to leave the Illinois Territory.

There were plenty of young soldiers willing to step into the captain's adulterous shoes, but no single one satisfied Mary's financial needs. Over time, the ever-increasing traffic of men in the vicinity of the young mother's cabin caught the attention of the women in the settlement, and eventually the wives at Fort Dearborn. An angry mob of fifteen ladies brandishing iron skillets and a musket or two converged on her cabin. They convinced Mary to pack up her possessions and leave.

"Help me," she begged the local blacksmith. "I need to borrow your wagon and horses to move my things."

"How far you going?"

"I don't care," she admitted. "Pretty far." She threw a fearful glance over her shoulder. "Do you know of a town that's big enough to need a seamstress?"

The blacksmith smirked. "Is that what you call it? Being a seamstress? That's why a mob of women came to your door?"

Mary blushed, but lifted her chin and met the blacksmith's gaze. "I can sew," she said.

"I'm sure you can." He dropped his tools and wiped both hands on his leather apron. "I'll help you load up your stuff, and I'll take you as far as LaSalle where I've got business to tend to. That's more than a day's ride, should be far enough to get you quit of your troubles. You'll have to make your own way from there. Maybe take a keelboat on down the Illinois to Peoria. Try to meet up with folks who would help you. Church folks, maybe."

She viewed the smithy's advice with disdain. Church folks made up most of the mob that ran her out of the settlement. They hadn't been of a mind to help. Mary went home to gather the few belongings that would fit in the blacksmith's buckboard and to prepare four-year-old Caswell for the move. She frequently opened her door a crack and peered outside, but no one came to bother her.

In Peoria on the Illinois River in December of 1818, a huge cheering crowd collected on the docks. Mary left the boat to see what the fuss was about. Illinois had just become a state and spirits were high. The mob of revelers shifted, flocking toward the nearest tavern. Mary, who held Caswell by his hand, stumbled dangerously close to the dock's edge. A strong arm clad in buckskin reached out to steady her, and a deep voice called, *"Faites attention."* Alerted to the risk, her balance secured by the man's strong arm, Mary and her son avoided a fall into the river.

When Mary responded in French to the bearded man in his backwoods garb, she saw his eyes light up and his mouth curve into a smile. She made up her mind in a split second and allowed Henri de Montagne, hunter and trapper, to escort her and her son back on board. He guided her to a bench and sat down beside her, asked where she was going and did she not have a traveling companion. Then he sat back and listened while Mary told him as much of her story as she wished to reveal. When she finished, she sat with her eyes downcast and her hands clasped demurely in her lap. She waited.

Henri remained quiet for a moment, then cleared his throat.

Mary glanced up hopefully. Henri squinted his eyes and

frowned. Fearing he now regretted helping her, Mary clutched her hands together and squeezed out a few tears to convince him of her need. She plucked a dainty handkerchief from her sleeve and dabbed at her eyes.

"Madame Proud, please, do not cry. I know of a village, but many miles inland and far to the south. I'm traveling to the west beyond the Mississippi." Henri spoke English with a heavy accent, softening the "th" to sound like a "z."

"I trap the beaver, you see," he continued, "and it has become difficult to find the beaver in Illinois. Too many people, too many buildings."

Mary donned her most soulful expression. She looked deeply into the man's eyes. "*Je comprends,*" she whispered. "I do understand, but . . ."

"It is necessary I reach the mountains before spring when the beaver and the bear come out of hibernation. I will have all the summer to hunt and trap."

Mary could tell he rambled now, that he weakened more each moment. It would take one little sob, then she could turn away and wipe her eyes . . . and he would be lost.

"But if you could help me, Monsieur de Montagne, I promise I will pay you back. You'd lose a little time, *c'est vrai*, but I won't keep you long. And when you come back to Illinois . . . you do plan to return, do you not? . . . You will always be welcome in my home. You will have a friend . . . a lady friend . . . to speak to you in your own language."

With those few words, Mary found a new benefactor.

Henri borrowed a wagon and used his two pack mules to take Mary and Caswell to the Village of Sangamon, certain, so he said, the kind community would take them into its heart. Mary welcomed the long move. The townsfolk of Sangamon lived much too far from Fort Dearborn to hear of her reputation.

★ ★ ★ ★ ★

The town's grocer, Jeremiah Frost, welcomed the newcomers to Sangamon on a freezing cold day in January of 1819. Jeremiah referred Mary to Sam Bench, the owner of the saloon, who rented her a tiny cabin he'd built when he first arrived in the territory. Constructed from a combination of logs and mud stucco, and sporting a new sod roof, the one-room dwelling at the edge of Sangamon bore no resemblance to anything Mary would call a house. But she'd survived worse, like the tent city near Fort Dearborn where cold winds from the lake ripped the camp apart during the winter. The log cabin would have to do. At least the walls were solid, a few pieces of furniture included, and the fireplace big enough to heat the whole room.

Henri carried her things inside, then dropped a small buckskin pouch into her hand, apologizing profusely for leaving again so soon. When he mounted the buckboard and disappeared on the road north, a cloud of dust was soon the only evidence he had been there at all.

Mary opened the bag and poured several coins and three tiny gold nuggets into her palm. She studied them a moment, then returned them to the pouch and shoved it into the pocket of her cloak. This bit of treasure would be hidden away, along with the money she'd received from her father. There were other ways to finance her day-to-day expenses.

Mary quickly discovered her landlord, Sam Bench, was a worldly man, but one devoutly faithful to his wife, a stern woman who watched her husband like a hawk, giving him little opportunity to stray. He did, however, acknowledge Mary's fluttering eyelashes and demure glances with a long wistful expression. Her vague references to her occupation as a seamstress, intended to give her an air of respectability, caused the man to sigh. Still, Mary's landlord kept his distance.

"There's more and more people coming through here every week," Sam told her. "Some passing through. Some coming to trade. They might have need of a seamstress now and then. And, Jeremiah back there, the one you talked to when you got to town, he's got problems with a sickly wife. He might need help." He turned to make eye contact with Mary. "In the store, I mean." He continued to hold Mary's attention until she understood what he wouldn't say out loud.

"How kind of you to tell me. I'll talk to him today," she said.

"And if I hear anyone else needs sewing done," the saloon-keeper added, "I'll send them your way."

Two days later Mary stood inside the general store's doorway, her hands still encased in her dirty fur muff. She peered into the store's dimly lit interior, her eyes blinded by the bright sun's reflection off the snow-covered land outside.

"Mr. Frost," Mary began, "I understand you might need assistance in your store?"

"No, I think not," answered a woman's voice.

Mary stepped further inside, squinting to see who had spoken. "You're Mrs. Frost?" she asked. "I'm sorry. I thought you were ill and could not work."

The grocer's wife waved her arm in dismissal. "Only a babe reluctant to find its way into this hard world. Now he squalls in protest at what he found, but a healthy squall it is. And I'm fit as a fiddle, as ye can see. Would ye be having anything else?"

"No . . . but I'm in need of work. I have a baby to care for. If there's ever a need for fancy needlework . . . I do sew."

"Ye and all the other women hereabouts. Not much call for fancy work a woman cannot do for herself. Maybe in the spring . . . farm work?"

Mary backed out the door and made her way back to her cabin through the snow. After checking to see if Caswell still slept, she draped her coat and muff over a chair. She pulled off her wet shoes and placed them near the fireplace to dry.

A nagging ache behind Mary's eyes intensified as it spread. She lay down on her bed, careful not to disturb Caswell, and closed her eyes.

Henri came back to Sangamon in October of that same year. As was the custom for frontier trappers, he made most of his own clothes, using deer hide and beaver or rabbit pelts. He had little need for a seamstress. When he left the wild country to do business with the civilized world, he needed only three things before he escaped back to his solitary life: quality whiskey, a hot bath, and a soft bed in a cozy room with a lady. If the lady occasionally sat nearby in her rocking chair, embroidering fine fabrics as she spoke to him softly in French, then Henri was even more satisfied.

He spent most of the profit from his fur trades to get these things. On his first trip back to see Mary, Henri surprised her with a fine set of embroidery needles, threads in assorted colors, and two embroidery hoops.

Henri appreciated the fact that Mary willingly offered her body in exchange for those gifts. He took full advantage of their arrangement, so it was no surprise to Mary when she became pregnant. By the time Henri began his spring preparations to head west, Henri knew she was expecting a child. Mary fantasized about the security of marriage. Henri, it seemed, fantasized about relocating to California.

A rapidly accelerating downhill slide in the relationship soon began. Mary had not forgotten the hardships she endured when she and David traveled from Philadelphia to Illinois. And now Henri expected her to go all the way to California in her condition, and in a covered wagon, and with a five-year-old boy as well? She begged him to stay, or at least to return each fall, but she was certain he'd marry her immediately, now that he knew she carried his child.

Henri said no. He would take her and Caswell along, but he was French and Catholic, and he could not divorce his wife who lived in Montpellier with his four sons and waited patiently for his return.

That revelation removed almost all signs of gentility and grace from Mary's appearance and behavior.

Henri left for Missouri in March, telling Mary he wanted to track down rumors of a great migration west and find out how he could participate. In June he came back and found a different Mary than the one to whom he'd become accustomed.

She did not welcome him with open arms. She did not speak to him softly in French. She hummed no sweet melodies. Instead, Mary met Henri at the door with a vitriolic verbal attack, and then threw an iron skillet at his head when he kicked off his moccasins to sit down in front of her fire. She lumbered toward the door, opened it wide, gestured for him to leave, and waited, her hands on her hips, her huge belly thrust defiantly forward.

Chapter Seven:
The Truth About Henri

Henri didn't mind leaving Mary. He gently rubbed his head where the skillet she'd thrown had left a fearsome bruise. What did it matter? His Sauk wife would welcome him when he caught up with the tribe at Saukenuk. And there were plenty of saloon wenches and widowed squaws who welcomed Henri's attentions and his full purse as he traveled west to the mountains.

When he'd first met Mary Proud, he couldn't believe his good fortune. A widow in need of protection and, if her flirtatious manner told the truth, one quite willing to provide a warm bed and open arms in return. Henri promptly fell in love, as he usually did when he met a beautiful and compliant female. He, of course, did not mention his squaw, or the family in Montpellier.

When he discovered Mary was pregnant with his child, he saw no reason why things should change, at least not until he left for good. His bastard children, white and Indian, could be found throughout the prairies and mountains of this vast country. What difference did one more make?

From time to time over the next twelve years, Henri returned from his hunting trips and renewed friendships in towns from St. Louis, Missouri, to Lafayette, Indiana. Occasionally he stopped along the Sangamon and spent time with his old friend, the Indian known as Fish.

When the weather was good, the two men sat on logs in the clearing in front of Fish's *wikiyapi*. Henri learned to speak Kickapoo. In return, he taught Fish a little French. Both spoke English, each with his own jumbled word choices and accent.

"You come with me, eh? I get you a mule, maybe two. We go west, find the beaver?"

Fish shook his head. "No, my friend. If I leave this place, I cross the big river and find where the soldiers took my people."

"Ah, yes. You know, there were many Kickapoo with Black Hawk at Bad Axe River."

Fish shrugged. "Foolish men who did not see past the next bottle of whiskey."

"Not many Kickapoo left."

"Kenekuk crossed the big river. Many Kickapoo went north, followed Kenekuk. Others went south. Kickapoo will not die."

At the sound of water splashing in the river, Henri jumped to his feet.

Fish waved him back. "That little girl, Jo Mae. She made friends with old dog. She talks, always talks, sometime talks to me, sometime talks to dog. She's a funny girl, a good girl. I know her from first day she was born."

"She lives in the village?"

"Mmm. Live with mother and no-good brother. You know," Fish added with a sly glance. "Mother's name is Mary Proud. Brother's name is Caswell. Little girl, Jo Mae."

Henri shook his head as though he'd never heard of them. Even though Fish made the girl's name sound more like Yo-may, Henri knew who she was. He'd heard the talk in the village. Jo Mae was his child. One glance at the Indian told him Fish also knew more than Henri would have liked. "*Peut-être* . . . perhaps. But the girl . . . *non, je ne pense pas.* I do not think I know her."

Fish motioned toward the river. "Go see."

Henri walked into the woods. When he drew near the splashing sounds, he slowed, staying behind the trees and bushes so he would not be seen. The girl scooped up handfuls of river water and poured them over the dog's mangy head. As Henri studied her face, he saw himself in her features. He backed away and returned to the clearing.

"You see?" asked Fish.

"Her brother is . . . how do you say no good?"

"Ugly in heart, ugly in head. When he was a small boy, he hurt the old dog, made him step in a trap, pushed a stick in the dog's eye. Now Jo Mae's brother is bigger than me, like a man, and he pushed me down. One day he kicked me in the head. I think an evil spirit lives in the heart of Caswell Proud."

"I do remember Caswell when he was five or six years. Quiet boy. Sat by Mary's side and did not talk. If she let him go out, he stayed out for many hours. I did not know he did anything wrong."

"I saw him pull Jo Mae's arm. One day he pinched her so hard, she screamed and cried."

Henri suspected Fish told him about Caswell's cruelty for a reason, hoping perhaps Henri would do anything to protect his child. But Henri had no desire to interfere and risk another confrontation with Mary.

As a matter of fact, Henri feared the possibility of Mary's capitulation more than anything else. Once far away from Mary's attentions and the comfort of her cabin, he realized the last thing he wanted was the responsibility and the burden of Mary and her children on a long wagon train journey to California. What would become of them when he returned to France?

Henri shook his head. "No, *mon ami*, I will not have any part of this little problem."

No expression of disapproval or disappointment showed on Fish's face.

Two days later, Henri climbed on his horse and rode away, confident he would have no future contact with Mary Proud or his daughter or Caswell.

CHAPTER EIGHT:
JO MAE GROWS UP

I must have been four years old or thereabouts the first time I saved something in my head that I can recollect even today. It was cold outside, but I got out the door without Mama seeing me, and I ran away. I had no shoes on, and no coat either, so I like to froze to death before Miz Frost saw me running past the store. She stopped me cold with one look, and then she told me to get home or she'd take a willow switch to my legs. Well, I did not know what a willow switch even felt like back then, and I did not know which way to go home, so I sat down in the middle of the road and started to cry.

About that time, Mama came marching down the road, and I knew I was in for a whipping, so I jumped up and took off running the other way. She caught me right quick and dragged me home, kicking and screaming all the way. By the time we got inside, I guess she was all tired out, because she did not do anything except latch the door up high so I could not reach it.

A bit later, Caswell banged on the door to get in. I ducked under the table because I was already afraid of Caswell by then. He treated me bad, even when I was little.

When I grew old enough to go to school, I was already wandering around town by myself. Sometimes I followed Caswell places, sneaking real quiet so he would not know I was there. I wanted to see him do something bad, so I could tell on him and get him thrown out of town.

Following Caswell is how I got down to the river for the first time and found out about Fish and his dog. Caswell watched them for a time, and I thought he went on home, but all of a sudden he jumped out of the woods and yelled at me. I let out a screech and tried to run away, but Caswell grabbed onto my foot. I fell into the bushes, and I was still screeching because the bushes hurt and because Caswell kept on kicking me.

All of a sudden, Fish stepped in between us, and the dog growled and moved slow like he was about to jump. He showed his teeth and ran after Caswell.

I never saw Caswell looking so afraid of anything until that day. His face got white and his eyes got big and he let out a screech of his own before he took off running.

Fish pulled me out of the bushes and brushed me off, saw I was not hurt much and said, "Come." He walked to where the woods stopped and he showed me the road. I did not see Caswell anywhere, so I ran as fast as I could back to Sangamon.

I got nothing but meanness from Caswell, at least until I turned twelve years old. After that, I learned things could happen to a little girl lots worse than getting pinched or hit.

CHAPTER NINE:
CASWELL SEIZES AN OPPORTUNITY

For the first few years after Jo Mae was born, Caswell ignored her most of the time. Even when she started walking and getting into things, she didn't bother him too much. He hid his secret things, like the dog's paw, in the big tree or buried them in the ground in the softer soil near the river, places she couldn't get to on her own.

The trouble began when Jo Mae grew old enough to leave the house without Mama. The stupid girl followed him everywhere. He'd climb his tree and she'd be down below, yelling his name. He'd go down to the river, and there she'd be. It made him madder than Miz Gray's rooster after Caswell hit it with a rock.

It didn't take long for him to figure out mean things he might do to make Jo Mae leave him alone. The old dog kept away from him now, ever since it lost its foot in the Injun's trap. But when he tried out his plan on Jo Mae, it didn't work the way he wanted it to. Jo Mae talked a whole lot better than the dog. Next thing, she ran to Mama, crying about how he pinched her arms black and blue. Telling on him when he tripped her and she fell face first into the mud. Screeching about him holding her head under muddy water at the river until she nearly drowned.

He learned it didn't matter much when Jo Mae told on him. At first he got yelled at and told to leave his sister alone. But after a while, mostly because Jo Mae never shut up, and partly because Mama would not believe all those stories Jo Mae told on him were true, Mama yelled more at Jo Mae about being a tattler than she did at Caswell for being mean. Mama said Jo Mae must have done something to deserve whatever she got.

"Stay away from him, Jo Mae," Mama would tell her. "If you didn't follow him around, tormenting him so, he'd leave you alone."

"I don't do anything to him, Mama. He's purely wicked through and through and will not leave me be."

"Oh, Jo Mae, shut your mouth. I can't listen to any more or I'll get one of my headaches. Go outside, or go talk to Annie Gray. Maybe she has chores you can do. And don't forget to mind your manners."

Caswell let the left side of his mouth curl up into an "I told you so" grin. Jo Mae clamped her lips closed, stuck her arms stiff as boards down at her sides, and made such tight little fists of her hands, her knuckles turned white. She gave him a hateful look, and without another word, she marched out the door, giving it a good hard slam as she left.

By the time Jo Mae was six years old, the other children knew her as that dirty little Proud girl. They mocked the way she ran around town, always watching over her shoulder like she had a wolf at her heels. They made fun of her grubby clothes and filthy bare feet, and ran away laughing when she threw rocks and sticks to make them stop. Caswell laughed and walked away.

By the time she was twelve, and the boys even older, she ran and fought to protect herself from things worse than mean words. The boys grabbed at her, trapping her in corners and pulling at her clothes, whispering and sneaking around so their folks wouldn't see. Jo Mae scratched and hollered like those boys wanted to skin her alive.

Caswell knew what was going on but didn't much care as

long as he didn't get blamed. He didn't care if Jo Mae got beat up. He didn't care if she bloodied a stupid farm boy's nose.

At first, he didn't understand what the grabbing and wrestling and struggling meant. When five of the boys overcame their fear of Caswell enough to ask his help in trapping Jo Mae so they could "look her over a bit," they surprised Caswell so much he was speechless as he tried to figure out what they were talking about.

The boys glanced at each other and took a step backward.

Caswell raised his hand to scratch his head. The closest boy flinched and took another step back.

"Why?" Caswell asked. "She isn't nothing to look at."

"She's a girl, ain't she?"

Caswell didn't get it. What did these boys, most of them younger than him, want with Jo Mae? Maybe it was their mama's idea, he thought. Like getting a girl to do the extra work—house cleaning and farm chores like Jo Mae did for Miz Gray.

"Well, she's strong for her size, but she can't cook, if that's what you're asking," Caswell told them.

The boys bent over laughing, then stood around a little longer, shuffling their feet. The same one who'd spoken before, the one who appeared to be the oldest, spelled out what they wanted. Then he stepped back, ready to run, in case Caswell got mad.

Caswell wasn't mad. He was confused. "Y'all want to see her naked?"

"Sure, we do," the oldest-looking boy said.

"What for?"

The boys burst out laughing again.

Caswell studied their faces, trying to put it together with anything he'd ever wanted to do with a girl, which was pretty near nothing. He thought back a few years, when Mama moaned and squirmed around in her bed with the trapper man that talked funny. If that kind of moaning and squirming was what the boys wanted, he guessed it was okay. He shrugged his shoulders. That part didn't matter much. He turned his mind to more important questions. Like would he get in trouble? And what would he get in return? By the time the trading was done, Caswell had three arrowheads, a hardtack biscuit covered with pocket lint, and a dried-up cow's eyeball.

At first he dragged Jo Mae behind the buildings where the boys waited for him to force Jo Mae to pull up her skirts. Next thing Caswell knew, he was catching her and pulling her into the woods so the boys could make her take all her clothes off. Caswell didn't keep track of whatever new shames the boys put on Jo Mae, and never figured out he could have fetched a higher price each time a boy tried something new.

Sometimes he wandered off, and sometimes he waited and watched. And he finally figured it all out when he saw three of the boys hold her down while a fourth lay on top of her with his pants pulled down. He bounced his hips up and down while Jo Mae hollered she would rip his guts out if he didn't stop hurting her. To Caswell, his little sister was such an awful creature he couldn't imagine wanting to even touch her except to beat her up. But he began to look at grown-up women in a different way, and sometimes his body did things that made him tingle all over and touch himself. He didn't tell anybody about that.

When one of the boys bragged about his adventures with Jo Mae to his older brother, the blacksmith, Colin Pritchard, who lived in town with his pregnant wife, the younger boys had to give up their fun. The older Pritchard whispered to Caswell he wanted some time with the girl. Caswell finally realized he could earn far more than useless junk and dirty food for bringing Jo Mae around.

He backed his sister into a corner and told her what she had to do. And she'd better do what he said, he told her, or he would cut her eyes out of her head. He showed her the dried cow's eyeball to make his point. When she put up her first fuss, he told her he'd tie her naked to a tree in the woods and let the snakes and wood rats eat her alive.

Caswell soon found most anything he wanted for himself or Mama could be traded for a few minutes of his sister's time. He liked apple brandy and homebrewed corn whiskey, so Caswell thought up the ugliest things he could do to Jo Mae, and then scared her with his awful talk every time she tried to fight back. One time, just to show her he meant what he said, he pulled up her dress and switched her bare legs with a willow whip, covering the skin with bloody stripes. He figured she knew he'd do it again, because no matter how hard she tried to get away, and how much she yelled to Mama, she always gave up in the end.

CHAPTER TEN:
JEREMIAH'S SIN

Jeremiah Frost was forty-seven years old when his young but worn-out wife sickened and declared herself done with child-bearing, housekeeping, and working in the general store. It took a couple of weeks for Jeremiah to understand this also meant the end of the lusty and frequently bawdy side of his marriage.

The last time he reached across his soundly sleeping wife, grabbed her breast, and gave it a playful squeeze, she promptly removed his hand and thrust it back to his own side of the bed. Astounded, he reached the same hand down under the covers and attempted to pull up his wife's nightgown. She kicked his hand away.

Jeremiah got the message, but he did not accept celibacy as an option. There being no whorehouse in the Village of Sangamon, Jeremiah considered the supply of widows and single women who might be agreeable to an arrangement of sorts.

His attempts to flirt with Annie Gray were met with a stony glare.

One stop at the schoolhouse with hat in hand and he reduced the schoolteacher, Sarah Wallace, to one of her frequent crying fits merely by suggesting he join her in her room for a cup of tea.

He next considered the widow Proud. Her past and her former relationship with the trapper, Henri de Montagne, were common knowledge. Even though she was no longer beautiful, nor did she take care with her appearance, she was most likely to benefit from a secret relationship and most likely the easiest to convince.

The Village of Sangamon had little more to offer. With a certain amount of resignation, Jeremiah knocked at Mary Proud's door late one evening.

Jo Mae pulled the door open and stood before him.

The whole interior of the cabin was visible from where Jeremiah stood. Mary lay in bed, her covers pulled over her shoulders. Caswell slumped in the rocking chair in front of the fire, but turned his head and stared with interest at the visitor in the doorway.

"What do you want?" asked Jo Mae.

"I came to see your mother . . . but I see this is not a good time."

Caswell pushed out of the chair and ambled across the room to face Jeremiah, looking him up and down. "You aiming to ask her for money? She owe too much at the store?"

"No, nothing like that."

Caswell shoved Jo Mae out of the way, planted himself in front of Jeremiah, and crossed his arms over his chest. "Then what?"

"I'll come back another time." Jeremiah backed away from the door, vowing to do no such thing.

"Wait," called out Jo Mae from behind Caswell's back. "I have not seen Miz Frost in the store for a time. Is she sick?" Jo Mae stepped out from behind Caswell and waited for Jeremiah to answer.

"My wife's feeling poorly. Can't work hardly at all. God bless our girls. They're doing the cooking and cleaning, and Benjamin helps tend the store. You know Ben? He's nearly your age, I'd guess."

Jeremiah looked into Jo Mae's brown eyes and caught his breath. Her lips were full and red, hints of the woman she would become. Her arms were slim and tanned, her ankles exposed, and her feet bare. Her breasts showed as tiny swells under the fabric of a dress that had grown too small.

Then Jeremiah realized what he'd said. This girl was no more than twelve years old, the same age as his youngest child.

"Well, I don't know anybody named Ben." Jo Mae lifted her chin and gave him a look that seemed defiant.

Jeremiah shifted his glance back to Caswell, who now stared at him with obvious interest.

"You wanting my mama to come down to the store tomorrow?" Caswell asked.

"No, no, that won't be necessary."

Caswell cocked his head to one side and grinned as though the purpose of the grocer's visit had now become perfectly clear.

Heat crept up from Jeremiah's neck to his face. He turned, stumbling on the step as he hurried away. The door slammed shut behind him.

In the next week, Caswell stopped by the store twice but left without buying anything or talking to anyone. On both occasions, Jeremiah was busy with customers, but did not fail to notice Caswell's odd entrance and immediate departure.

Toward the end of that week, the young smithy, Colin Pritchard, stopped in the general store and plopped down in one of the chairs Jeremiah had placed in the corner by the stove.

"Your wife feeling better now?" Jeremiah asked.

"She surely is. She's eating like she's storing up for a long winter."

"My wife only got sick like that with the first one. Lasted near four months. After that, with the other four, she wasn't sick at all."

Both men glanced toward the door as Jo Mae ran inside. She

saw Colin Pritchard sitting in the corner and came to an abrupt halt.

Pritchard froze, then turned and stared at the floor, bending over as though searching for something.

Jo Mae turned around and dashed out the door.

Jeremiah had observed the two with interest, and now looked at Pritchard as he asked, "You know that girl?"

"Nope."

"You know her brother, Caswell Proud? The bad one?"

"I reckon everybody knows him."

"You have any dealings with him?"

Pritchard flushed. "What do you mean?"

Jeremiah shrugged.

Pritchard stood up. "Guess I better be going. Wife'll be yanking on the bell rope if I don't get back soon with her cornmeal." He walked over to the counter and picked up the package, saying only, "Thank you kindly," as he left. He did not make eye contact with Jeremiah.

The grocer was not a stupid man. He had to make a decision, and it should be made before he saw Caswell again. Alone for the moment, he came around the counter and sat down in the chair recently vacated by Colin Pritchard. On the one hand, Caswell's young sister should not be treated like a whore. On the other hand, the family was destitute and needed to survive. Just because Caswell wouldn't take on work like a man was no reason his mother and sister should starve. Jeremiah could provide many benefits to the family in return for the discreet satisfying of his needs.

He wondered whether Jo Mae cooperated, or whether she had to be held down and forced. He cringed at the thought of such evil being brought down on his own daughters. Still . . . Jeremiah stood and stamped his feet, then walked back behind his counter and busied himself counting tins of snuff.

That evening, after dark, he announced to his wife he would take a stroll while he smoked his pipe. She, who claimed the smoke made her eyes water, waved him on his way without a second thought.

Jeremiah never lit his pipe. He found a spot under a tree near the Proud cabin and waited for nearly an hour. When no one appeared, he went home.

His new nightly ritual continued for two weeks before he saw the Proud's door open and Caswell peer outside, disappear back into the cabin for a moment, and finally come out, dragging Jo Mae by the hand.

The girl tried to pull away, kicked at Caswell's legs, and yelled at him. He turned and slapped her hard across the face. She kicked him again. He bent her arm behind her back and pushed her along in front of him.

When Caswell and Jo Mae were well ahead, Jeremiah followed. Caswell shoved Jo Mae into the dark space between the stable and the smithy's forge. Jeremiah stopped in the shadows across the road and waited. Moments later, he saw Colin Pritchard slip through the darkness. Almost immediately, Caswell came out of the shadows and sauntered down the road toward his mother's cabin.

Jeremiah dared go no closer. He waited. In less than five minutes, Jo Mae ran from the space between the stables and the forge. He could not see her face in the dark. She made no sound except for the pounding of her bare feet on the dirt road.

When Pritchard appeared, Jeremiah stepped out of the shadows, pulled out his pipe, struck a match on the rough bark of a tree, and lit his tobacco. Pritchard stopped and waited.

"Colin Pritchard," Jeremiah called out as he strolled toward the younger man.

Pritchard stood still, his shoulders slumped and his head bowed.

"You do conduct business with Caswell Proud, then."

Pritchard did not answer.

Jeremiah walked away.

The next day, Jeremiah saw Caswell on the street and asked him to stop by the store that afternoon, just before closing time. His meeting with Caswell was short. Before locking the door and heading home, Jeremiah wrapped two chunks of rock candy in paper and shoved them in his pocket.

That evening, when he left his cabin to take a late stroll and smoke his pipe, the package rubbed against his thigh and triggered a tingling in his loins. By the time he reached the dark alley between the stable and the forge, Jeremiah was trembling.

Caswell and Jo Mae had arrived before him. Jo Mae lay flat on her back, with Caswell straddling her. He held one hand over her mouth while he attempted to fight off her flailing arms and legs with the other.

"Come on," Caswell whispered. "You take her."

Jeremiah knelt next to Jo Mae and pulled the candy out of his pocket. "I won't hurt you," he whispered. "See what I brought?"

Jo Mae stopped kicking her legs and tried to push up on her elbows so she could see. She grabbed Caswell's hand and pulled it off her mouth.

"Who is it? Help me, Mr. Frost. Get Caswell off me!"

"Let her go," Jeremiah ordered.

Caswell snickered. "If I let her go, she'll run. But you pay. A deal's a deal."

"I don't care; let her go."

Jo Mae rolled over as Caswell pushed himself off and stood up. She rose into a crouched position, but instead of running, she leaned forward and peered intently at Jeremiah.

"Look," he said. "I brought you a present."

Caswell laughed and walked away.

"Wait," Jeremiah said. "I want you to bring her back tomorrow."

"More whiskey, a full cup this time."

Jeremiah shrugged. "A whole jar if you want." He turned his back on Caswell and focused his attention on Jo Mae.

"What do I have to do for that?" she asked.

"This time? Nothing. But he'll bring you back here tomorrow night. If you'll be quiet, no hollering and no fighting . . . if you'll be quiet and never tell, I'll be very nice. I'll bring you things you want. And I won't hurt you."

Jo Mae crouched silently before him for a minute or two, then reached out and took the rock candy from his hand.

Jeremiah continued with his arrangement, as time and weather allowed, over the next year. Because he treated Jo Mae with kindness, she gave him little trouble, even though she continued to fight Caswell up to the very second Jeremiah made his appearance.

Things changed during the late summer of 1833.

"I have not been with anybody but you more than three months now," Jo Mae told Jeremiah. "Nobody else, ever since that Pritchard baby got born and her daddy went back to bothering his own wife."

"Are you certain you're with child?"

"Yes, I'm sure. My mama figured it out before I even knew it."

"There's ways to make it go away, Jo Mae."

She laughed. "Go away? You mean, make it disappear like it never happened? Are you making fun of me?"

"No, not at all. There are leaves and seeds; the Indians use them. You chew them up—"

"There's nothing that will make me hurt this baby, Mr. Frost." Jo Mae scooted away from Jeremiah and looked him in the eye. "And since it's sure enough yours, you've got to help me. You tell Caswell you are not going to have anything more to do with me, and you tell him I can't go with anybody else."

Nothing he said would change her mind. He could not enlist anyone else's help to convince her. At least Jo Mae didn't threaten him with exposure, but he wondered what she would be forced to tell her mother and others who would know soon enough. He wanted to say more to Jo Mae, but as he tried to put his thoughts together, she spoke again.

"I will not talk to you any more, Mr. Frost, unless I have to come into the store for my mama. Folks might get funny ideas and get to whispering around town and that would be pitiful sad for Miz Frost and those kids you have. You talk to Caswell real soon, like I said."

Jeremiah did as he was told. Guilt and fear of exposure hovered over his head every moment of the day. He remained concerned about Caswell, especially if he deprived the boy of his drink. When he told Caswell the bad news about Jo Mae, Jeremiah softened the blow with a jar of brandy and the promise of more to come. It was the prudent thing to do.

The swarm of worries hummed even louder when the preacher returned. Once again, Jeremiah extended the welcome, set up the bible meeting, and attended the gathering with his wife and children, all the time trying to brush away the buzzing in his brain that made him dizzy.

Jeremiah prayed, as he'd never prayed before, that a miracle would happen to prevent his life, and the lives of his wife and children, from spinning out of control.

Chapter Eleven:
About the Preacher's Calling

John Claymore, an ordained Presbyterian minister, rode a circuit that took him throughout central Indiana and Illinois. He refused to carry a gun. God had called him into His service, and God would protect him from wild animals, hostile Indians, outlaws, and demons.

In January of 1833, as he approached the Village of Sangamon for the first time, he thought of the good news he'd heard in the last town to the north. His old friend from New Salem would run again for the Illinois House of Representatives. It had been two years since the election loss that might have given a less determined man than Abraham serious doubts about his future in politics. This time, John was confident his friend would win.

When he reached the village center, John tied his brown and white pinto to the railing in front of the Sangamon General Store and Trading Post. The village was small; he'd guess maybe fifteen or twenty log cabins. A few were larger than average with painted signs hung above the doors. Most storefronts were neglected, the signs so faded they were barely legible.

One of the smaller cabins at the far end of the main road had a bell on a post outside the door and a rope swing dangling from one heavy branch of a huge tree. Apparently there were enough children from the village and surrounding farms to justify at least a part-time teacher, who most likely worked for room and board and perhaps, if he was lucky, a very small wage.

81

Real money was a scarce commodity in this part of the country.

John paused at the doorway of the general store and peered inside. A woman wearing a long gray dress and bonnet gave precise instructions to the storekeeper as he measured flour and cornmeal with a scoop and poured them into the small muslin bags she handed him.

Three men, dressed in brown homespun shirts worn thin at the elbows and blue denim pants tucked into their scuffed boots, played cards at a table in the corner, their rickety wooden chairs creaking each time they shifted their weight. They must have purchased their clothing at the same time and place, John thought. A small pile of dried corn sat in front of each player which led the preacher to believe the men were gambling.

Tools of every sort, many of them handcrafted, hung from the walls. The room smelled of vinegar, salted meat, and tobacco—comfortable warm odors that reminded John of home.

Everyone turned when John walked into the store. He removed his hat. "I'm John Claymore, preacher for the Presbyterian denomination, but eager to make the acquaintance of all good people in Sangamon, be ye Presbyterian or other."

The three men stuffed their cards in their boots, brushed the piles of corn onto the floor, and jumped to their feet. They surged forward to shake John's hand as though greeting the most welcome visitor to come to the Village of Sangamon in years.

And that may well be true, thought John, although he knew the men were usually less interested in sermons and bible meetings than were the women. If they were only pretending to welcome him to town, the men did a convincing job of it. John glanced over at the table, and at the scattered corn on the floor. *Think of it; my mere entry into a room can banish sin.*

The woman in the gray dress finished her shopping and turned toward the preacher. Before she could speak, they heard a noise at the door. A young girl—little more than eleven or twelve in John's estimation—rushed in and dashed up to the counter. She wore an old coat that hung to her ankles, and she kept pushing up the sleeves, revealing her dirty, ungloved hands.

"Headache powders," she said. "Mama says she'll pay you when she can."

The storekeeper started to answer, glanced at the preacher who stood close enough to hear the conversation, then sighed and turned to the shelves behind him, moving several small boxes aside to get to the one he wanted.

The girl jumped from one booted foot to the other while she eyed the strings of rock candy that hung from the ceiling over the scales. When the storekeeper finally handed her the tiny paper packet, she thanked him properly, gave one last wistful glance at the candies, and then clomped out the door without acknowledging any of the store patrons.

John watched her depart, then again faced the counter. "Poor child. Is her family in great need?"

The storekeeper shook his head. The lady in the gray dress sniffed and pursed her lips. She grabbed up her navy blue cloak from the counter and put it on, turned her back on the preacher, and left the store. As they hurriedly pulled on their coats, the three men began a slow exodus toward the door, ignoring John's question about the girl. Each man said he'd fetch his wife and children to meet the new preacher and promised to spread the word.

The storekeeper was the only one left in the store. He arranged for John's bed and board for the next two evenings and a gathering place for John's prayer meeting. Jeremiah Frost, as the storekeeper introduced himself, assured John his services were sorely needed in Sangamon.

"Hasn't been a preacher hereabouts for near a year," Frost said, "not since that fire and brimstone Methodist who nearly scared the whole town to death with his ranting."

"I assure you, I will frighten no one."

"Not that a few of us couldn't do with a touch of holy guidance—"

"That you'll have." *A good man,* John told himself. *Town leader, no doubt.*

"What news do you bring, Reverend?"

"You know about the plan to clear the Sangamon River, make it usable for flatboats and such?"

"Aye. A crazy idea conjured up by that Lincoln boy who tried to get elected to the legislature. Nothing will come of it."

"Landowners over in Champaign County are getting assessed land taxes this year," said John. "First time ever."

Jeremiah glared as though he would hold John personally responsible if such a thing were to happen in Jeremiah's county.

John changed the subject. "Folks are swarming into the state like a plague of locusts since Black Hawk's been captured. Did you know they locked him up over in Jefferson Barracks?"

"At St. Louis. Imagine that. After all the killing that savage did, you'd think they would've hanged him."

John thought of things he could say about the unfair and often brutal treatment the northern tribes had received at the hands of land-and-riches-seeking white people on the move. Instead, he changed the subject again.

"You say I go straight through the town to the blacksmith shop?"

"He'll put you up. You tell him I sent you. And if you go on through the town to the farm at the far end, there you'll find Miz Annie Gray. She's a good Christian woman. She'll help you organize your meeting."

John, pleased with the welcome extended to him upon his arrival and encouraged by the prompt attention to his requirements, concluded he would find his visits to Sangamon most fulfilling. And with a little kindly persuasion, perhaps he could soften Mr. Frost's pessimism.

Although John's religious indoctrination had begun as soon as he was old enough to accompany his parents to church, the assault on his soul did not begin until 1814, when he was seven years old. In May of that year, his mother lost her youngest child, an eighteen-month-old boy, when he fell in the river near Galena and drowned. Determined to protect her remaining child at all costs, Mrs. Claymore promised God if He'd allow young John to grow into manhood, strong and healthy, she would hand her son into His service.

After that, John sat with his mother in the tiny church nearly every day. Often they were the only ones in the room.

"He told me Himself," she repeated often. " 'Young John was born under a holy sign.' "

"Who told you, Mother?"

"He told me Himself," she repeated, astonished the child kept asking the same question over and over. "You belong to Him. You will be His voice in this desperate land. Now bow your head."

John leaned his head against his mother's arm and shut his eyes as she began to pray.

Master Bryson, John's undergraduate academic advisor and a staunch atheist, had groomed the brilliant young John Claymore to study law. Bryson was not easily put off when creating one of his master plans for another man's life and career. Because of his vision for John's future, Bryson even withheld his letter of recommendation when he found the lad applying to divinity school instead of law school. When that did not produce the desired result, Bryson traveled from Connecticut to Illinois at considerable expense and loss of time from his own pursuits, to talk to his errant protégé's father.

"The boy does not have a true calling," stated Master Bryson, although he neglected to mention he thought the whole idea of a *calling* total nonsense. Correctly assuming the elder Claymore was a religious man himself, Bryson did not reveal his own tendencies to ridicule primitive devotion to an unproven and unlikely deity.

"Not a true call of God that would make John a great minister to the poor wretched souls who cry out for salvation," Bryson continued. "But he's determined. Nothing I say will change his mind. I hope you'll be my ally in this cause, that you'll help me dissuade John from what could be a horrible mistake."

John's father shifted in his chair, wondering how his son had tolerated this pompous man as his advisor, and whether the instructors at the Presbyterian seminary would also be overbearing. He couldn't think of anything to say.

Bryson quickly took advantage of the silence. "He's like so many other young men. Someone put this notion into his head, a missionary no doubt, and now he's going to proceed with his idealistic vision no matter what anyone else says. I'm sure you've done your best to talk him out of seminary?" Bryson raised his eyebrows and waited briefly for Claymore to respond, then took the man's shrug as agreement and continued.

"Then you know what I mean. Well, what can you do?" Bryson rambled on, oblivious to Claymore's growing irritation. "The seminary accepted your boy in spite of my strong reservations and without my personal or academic recommendation. I suppose they're desperate for young men who are willing to ride the prairies and brave the dangers of the wilderness. A special breed . . . like missionaries. They think they're off to a great adventure . . . save souls, fend off the devil, get themselves to Heaven."

Afraid Bryson was about to launch into another long-winded

lecture, Claymore pulled his pocket watch out by its chain and glanced at it, then stood. "My word! I had no idea of the time. I'm so sorry, but I have an appointment. I hope you'll forgive me."

Bryson started to speak, but Claymore hurried out the door before Bryson could protest.

John, waiting outside, jumped up as his father strode briskly into the hall. "I heard every word," he said as he ran to keep up. "It's confirmed, then. Master Bryson has not been able to prevent my admission to seminary."

"It's true. What an arrogant old fool he is. Coming all this way to consult with me, when he knows full well you've already made up your mind. And you being emancipated. Did the insufferable old goat think I would take a strap to you so you'd see the error of your ways?"

"I no longer have to endure the teachings of Master Bryson, Father. He'll be in Connecticut, still preaching the law as though revealing the Ten Commandments. And I'll be at Western Seminary in Pennsylvania, attending to my studies. I'll be a Presbyterian preacher, whether Master Bryson approves or not. God has summoned me to his side, chosen me out of so many men who aspire to serve. I will heed His call."

The elder Claymore stopped and placed his hand on John's shoulder. "A fine preacher you'll be, John. But cleanse your sermons of the rigid and harsh doctrines we're accustomed to hearing. If you must do your mother's will, be a refreshing voice amongst the dour old men who threaten eternal damnation for doing almost anything God put us on this earth to enjoy. Your mother tends to—"

"I know, Father. She's devout in the old way. But you have influenced me as well. You helped me see a more gentle way to bring the flock back to the Holy Shepherd. I'll not forget what you've told me."

Claymore clapped John on the shoulder. "Don't forget the wolves and the mountain lions, John. They require a different approach. You must adapt to your surroundings." He chuckled. "Can you imagine your haughty Master Bryson facing off against a band of heathen Indians?"

In the summer of 1833, six months after his first visit to Sangamon, John again approached the village, this time traveling from southwestern Illinois. The last few months had taken him through late winter snows and early spring floods as he rode from farm to farm in the sparsely populated region. Once he reached the winding Sangamon River, he was back in familiar territory. He slowed his horse to a walk as he felt a breeze freshen the summer heat. He pulled his kerchief from around his neck and removed his hat to mop the sweat from his forehead.

Near the river, close to the edge of town, John heard a splash in the water and glanced down the muddy bank. The same girl he'd seen in the store in January now stood in the river, staring up at him. Her skirts were pulled up to her knees, her spindly bare legs apart, planted in the water as though she'd grown roots in the thick muck on the bottom. A mangy dog that looked as though it had been fighting wolves stood fiercely by the girl with its hackles raised. Its low rumbling growl was barely audible, but most definitely aimed at John.

The girl didn't speak to him, but tucked her skirt between her knees and bent down, using her hands to swish the water around her feet.

John let the pinto rest a minute longer as he sat and allowed the scene's tranquility to quiet his mind. *God dwells in this place. I feel Him here.*

★ ★ ★ ★ ★

Less than ten minutes later, as he approached the front of the
feed store in Sangamon, John unexpectedly came face to face
with a man whose eyes bored into his own as though tunneling
toward his soul. The man did not greet him with words, nor did
he smile. John's skin prickled and hairs lifted, even on his arms.
He flushed and tried to ward off the man's intrusive stare by
ignoring it.

The one thing he never expected to find in friendly, peaceful
Sangamon, population one hundred and twenty-seven, was a
man who wished harm on others, one perhaps capable of inflict-
ing harm if he were in the mood. John had noticed the type in
other towns—scoundrels hanging around saloons, robbing
banks, stealing horses—but not here. After his first visit to Sangamon, the preacher had designated the village, at least in his
own mind, a safe haven.

John rode past and kept his gaze forward.

What a disappointment, he thought. Sangamon, a community
of grace and strength and love. A place where he could find
kindness, acceptance, and a pious congregation to listen to his
sermons, sing hymns with enthusiasm, and pray with him.

Now this man . . . who was he? When did he arrive? Why was
he here?

Lost in thought, mulling over the distress he felt at this newly
discovered flaw in Sangamon's character, John urged his horse
toward the blacksmith's cabin where he was to sleep that night.
He had every intention of shrugging off the uneasy moment,
but when John described his experience, the blacksmith
grimaced and averted his gaze.

"Well, now that would be young Caswell, I reckon. He lives
with his ma and little sister, down by the schoolhouse."

The blacksmith did not elaborate.

"What's Caswell's family name?"

"I reckon that would be Proud." The blacksmith sniggered, still not looking the preacher in the eye. "That be a fitting name for lots of folks, but I reckon something got lost between the name and this family because . . ."

"Because?"

"I guess I shouldn't be talking about folks in a spiteful way, Preacher. But it's best to cut clear of Caswell. He can be a bad one when he's a mind to. You don't want him taking a dislike to you, if you know what I mean."

"They moved here recently?" asked John.

"Oh, no sir. They've been here near all Caswell's life. And he's been making trouble nigh on that long. There's plenty of folks here who would just as soon see that boy and his whole family gone forever. Would help them on their way if need be."

What else did I miss about Sangamon? John wondered. *Who else in this village suffers but I did not see?*

In spite of the blacksmith's warning, it was the preacher's mission to seek out those in need of salvation, not avoid them.

John lifted his chin and squared his shoulders. God would lead him to all those who had need of His Word. God surely put Caswell Proud in his path for that very reason. Most likely the man had no bad intentions; most likely he suffered from a darkness inside—a need to find the Light. In spite of all he'd been taught about the struggle between Good and Evil, and even though he'd observed many rough characters from a distance, John had never knowingly faced an evil person, and, frankly, doubted the existence of hell and its occupants.

One little corner of John's mind recalled the teaching that claimed Satan dwelt in darkness. *Such silliness,* he admonished himself. *Caswell Proud is just a man—nothing more and nothing less.*

CHAPTER TWELVE:
JO MAE AND THE QUESTION OF GOOD AND EVIL

That day after I saw the preacher and Caswell giving each other the eye, I ran home, wondering what Caswell would say to Mama.

"Jo Mae, how many times—?"

"I know, Mama. Don't slam the door. I won't do it again." Mama came at me, so I ducked and ran past her to the other side of her rocking chair so she could not catch me. "Mama?"

"What?" Now Mama was screaming as loud as a rabbit caught in a trap. I figured it was as good a time as any to ask the same question I'm always asking, but Mama never answers.

"Mama, who was my pa?"

This time I thought Mama was going to bust something in her head, because she got as red as one of Miz Gray's tomatoes. She grabbed hold of the arm of that rocking chair and jerked it clear across the room. I decided it would be good to talk about something different.

"Mama, there's a bible meeting at the schoolyard tonight. That preacher said I should go and bring my family and—"

"A bible meeting? You want to go to a bible meeting?"

Well, that did indeed turn Mama's attention away from me asking about who my daddy was. She started laughing like she was going to bust. Her face turned red again, but then she started choking, and of course that was my fault too, so she tried to give me a big slap on the head. She hardly touched me because I fell right down on the floor to get away, and then I scrambled out the door like one of those crawdads down by the river.

It is truly a wonder that I got all my wits and that none of my body parts have been broken with all the pushing and hitting and pinching that went on over the years. It is certain that if it was not for Miz Wallace the schoolteacher and Miz Gray, I would have a head full of nothing but bad thoughts.

Now it is true that I did not learn much reading, only a few parts of the Holy Bible, but Miz Gray showed me the words so many times I knew them as good as can be. And I hid those books Miz Wallace gave me under Mama's bed. And while I did not know how to write the alphabet yet, I knew what good manners were because Mama told me over and over. And I think I mostly knew what was right and what was wrong.

I knew that everything Caswell did to me, and what he made me do, was bad. I did not know if that made me as bad as Caswell. I did not think so, but there was not anybody to ask. The other thing I did not know for sure about was Mr. Jeremiah Frost. He was nice as could be and never hit me, and he gave me rock candy and sometimes even real food like a biscuit with meat inside. But he had a wife and children and still gave Caswell whiskey to bring me back behind the stable. So I thought that maybe sometimes being bad or being good was not so easy to figure out.

It did make me wonder if this was something the preacher knew and maybe could tell me about if I ever got to go to a bible meeting.

Chapter Thirteen:
Caswell at the Bible Meeting

"Mama, I'm going to the prayer meeting," said Caswell. "Are you coming?"

She stopped rocking and glared at him. "Don't be ridiculous. I don't need the whole town staring at me, whispering about my misfortunes. And Jo Mae doesn't need to be down there, either. It'll get people talking about her again. You see her, you send her back here."

"I will." His lower lip curled up as he pictured his sister crying in pain when he twisted her arm and pulled her toward home.

"I don't know why you're going to that meeting anyway," Mama added. "All they'll do is sing hymns, and then the preacher will give a long, boring sermon about going to hell if you don't change your ways. He'll make everyone promise to be good ever after and then he'll pray for so long, people will begin to feel like 'ever after' is way too long to commit themselves."

"I know, Mama. But the preacher himself called out to me when he rode into town today. I reckon it won't do no harm to see what he wants." Caswell grinned, thinking of the scared expression he'd put on that preacher's face by giving him the evil eye. He liked scaring people. "Maybe he'll set me on the path to redemption, Mama. Maybe he'll even save my soul."

Mama didn't notice Caswell's smirk and the sassy tone in his voice. She leaned forward and waved her finger at him, squinting her eyes and frowning.

"There's nothing wrong with the condition of your soul. The path to redemption need only be walked by those who have committed grievous sins. It's no sin to be poor, no matter how those high and mighty people behave. Now you go on. And if that preacher starts praying over you, tell him God needs to give us a lot more than a little redemption. Tell him we need food and clothes, and a bit of fixing up on this falling down old cabin."

"Yes, Mama."

"And remember, don't let that preacher get anywhere near Jo Mae. I don't want her talking to outsiders."

"I know, Mama."

Caswell rolled his eyes and left the cabin before Mama gave him any more orders about Jo Mae. He had something on his mind that involved only the preacher, and he didn't want anybody getting in his way.

He strode toward the school where the prayer meeting was about to start. A faint rumble in the southwestern sky caused him to glance over his shoulder. Off in the distance, a line of bluish-black clouds hung low to the ground. As the sun moved slowly downward, it turned the dark cloud tips a muddy pink. Flashes of light popped above the distant trees. Heat lightning. He went on, watching for Jo Mae while he kept an eye out for the preacher.

In the schoolyard, hay bales and boards laid across tree stumps served as sitting places for the town folks. Up in front, right next to the post with the school bell on it, sat a wooden chair Caswell guessed must be for the preacher. He hung back and waited.

Miz Gray, who acted like she was better than most folks, walked up the road alongside the preacher. They moseyed through the schoolyard, stopping to greet every single man and woman. The preacher shook hands, and patted little children on the head. He even stopped and prayed over the bald-headed Pritchard baby like he thought his prayers were going to make it grow hair.

Caswell shook his head and walked over to the huge tree at the edge of the schoolyard. He wasn't going to sit with the rest of those folks.

He leaned against the tree trunk, straight in front of where the preacher was trying to get everyone settled down. Folks bowed their heads all at the same time. Folded their hands together and pressed them to their chests. There was quiet except for the shuffling of feet and the quickly shushed voice of a small child.

The preacher closed his eyes and bowed his head and prayed a whole story Caswell couldn't make head or tail of. When the preacher finally got around to saying "Amen," it sounded sad, like he was sorry he had to stop praying and start sermonizing.

Before Caswell had a chance to get restless, he saw Jo Mae out of the corner of his eye. She snuck up from the road, walking slow and quiet like she thought nobody would notice. He grabbed at her hair before she could get away.

"Here you are. After Mama told you not to. Don't you know you'll go to hell if you don't do what Mama says? Burn in a fire that lasts forever."

"That's not so," Jo Mae yelled.

Caswell wanted to give the preacher another fright, but first he had to follow Mama's orders and get Jo Mae home. Instead, Jo Mae's yelling got the preacher's attention, so now he had a reason to point at Caswell and get everyone in the schoolyard to turn and stare.

Like that Pritchard boy, staring at Caswell like he was the only one who ever done something bad. And old Jeremiah Frost, with his nose in the air. They'd sure enough be scared if Caswell stood up there with the preacher and told what they'd been doing with Jo Mae.

CHAPTER FOURTEEN:
JO MAE AT THE BIBLE MEETING

I did go down to that bible meeting that evening. There was a big crowd of people, even some of those folks I thought would be too ashamed, and some from the farms who did not come to Sangamon much, because they said the town and the river smelled bad and they called us river rats and said other mean things.

That preacher did not sound like other preachers we had visit for revivals and prayer meetings, like the ones who shouted and carried on about the fire in hell that lasts forever. When I heard those words, I always worried about the poor souls who hopped around trying not to get burnt to a crackling.

This time there was not any yelling and carrying on. The air was quiet and soft in the schoolyard, and folks were listening to the preacher's words like they'd never heard a preacher before. I kept on creeping closer and closer so I could hear, but I had trouble understanding, so I mostly listened to the sound of the preacher's voice and watched his mouth move and watched his eyes as he looked at people and talked right to them. The next thing, like it happened in some kind of dream, he looked into my eyes and said words right at me, and I thought I would melt into a puddle.

"Evil is all around us, trying to steal our souls and lead us away from God," he said. "But God wants us to chase that evil out of our lives. How do we do that? We chase the evil away by loving the Lord in our hearts and by turning our backs on evil thoughts and evil deeds."

The preacher had put his clenched fist against the middle of his chest while he was talking to me. I put my own hand on my swollen belly and wondered if he knew I had a child growing in there, and I wondered if I should not be wishing so hard that Caswell would die and go to hell. And then I wondered what God and the preacher would think of me if they had any idea what I was doing back there behind that stable. I wondered if maybe God would want to punish me instead of watch over me, and I wondered at how much evil there might be in this world since that preacher was talking about it so much.

Just when I was trying to figure all that out, Caswell grabbed me and jerked me around. He whispered at me in a nasty voice, "What are you doing here, Jo Mae Proud? You don't need to listen to him. You get on home now or the devil will come and drag you down into the fire."

"That is not so," I yelled, even if that very thing would get in my thinking sometimes and scare me near to death.

The preacher stopped preaching as soon as Caswell grabbed me. "Brother Caswell Proud," he called out. "It's good to see you here at our bible meeting. Why don't you sit down with these other fine folks and listen to the Word of the Lord?"

I did not know how the preacher knew my brother's name, but I could see that Caswell got real mad when everybody looked at us. His face went all red and his eyes squinted into little slits. You could hear the sss-sss-sss that said folks were whispering and acting all high and mighty like we were the only bad people in the Village of Sangamon. Caswell jerked on my elbow again and started to pull me away, and he did not say one word to that preacher. I turned back to see what the preacher was doing, and he had the saddest look on his face. But he surely did not try to save me, and because I could not do anything to save myself, I let Caswell drag me along home where he opened the door and pushed me inside. Then he took off again.

Mama had not gotten out of bed to see what was going on or screamed at me, so I thought she must be asleep. Of course, I snuck right back out the door and followed Caswell up the street. When he got near the school, he wandered around the edges of where the town folks were sitting. He finally settled on leaning up against a big old oak tree, which people say is the biggest and oldest oak tree anywhere around these parts. I thought Caswell was probably up to a whole passel of no good.

The preacher pointed at Caswell and told him again he ought to come on down front and be saved by the Lord, and Caswell made an ugly face like he smelled something rotten.

Folks were still turning around and staring and making those little whispery noises. Even Miz Gray and Miz Wallace were watching, and they did not hardly ever look hard on Caswell purely out of being scared plumb silly that he'd do something bad to them.

And then, with no warning at all, because I had not seen the clouds coming up and there'd been no rumbles or lightning, all of a sudden a loud booming noise made me jump about a hundred feet. Before that noise was gone, Caswell fell over in a big lump. The top of the oak tree was full of fire, and a big black mark curled down and around that tree all the way to where Caswell had been standing not one minute before.

Folks mostly shot up like they'd been stung by a bee and ran away to the schoolhouse. The preacher did not run away, and he did not look one bit afraid. He walked along toward Caswell as calm as could be, and when he got next to him, the preacher knelt down and put his fingers on Caswell's wrist.

"He's alive," the preacher shouted. "Is the doctor in town? Get the doctor over here."

Everybody ran every which way to find the doctor, so I did not wait any longer but ran home to tell Mama.

There was no accounting for how and why things happened the way they did. I could not understand why the lightning did not kill Caswell or at least set him on a path of goodness, especially since the preacher came to our house, acting like he really gave a hoot about Caswell living or dying. That was a mite peculiar when it was the preacher himself who'd struck Caswell down. Mama let the preacher in to do whatever praying he wanted to do, while she looked him up and down and sort of pranced around and acted nice.

Nothing good came of that visit. The preacher never said much more than two words to Mama, and the praying he did over Caswell did not do any good. I got to thinking maybe the preacher did not mean what he was praying. Maybe, like with the lightning, it only got done halfway.

CHAPTER FIFTEEN:
JOHN'S ARROGANCE AND AGONY

For those who sat in the schoolyard with their backs to the west, the darkening sky had signaled a rapidly approaching dusk. John Claymore was the only one who had a clear view of the clouds and the lights that flickered there. He ignored them. Instead, he focused on the task at hand—feeding the cravings of folks who were hungry for hope and starving for salvation.

John felt the energy growing inside his chest. God was gathering Himself into a force, ready to burst out of John in oratory that would smother the fires of hell, if indeed they existed. John wouldn't let Him down. John heard his voice grow louder. His hands reached out to the townsfolk as though to send God's Word through his own fingertips.

"We are taught the secret path to God," John told them. "That path is through love. The bible says 'Beloved, let us love one another: for love is of God; and everyone that loveth is born of God, and knoweth God.' But what happens to us in the absence of love, whether it be love of God or love of fellow man? There is jealousy. Pride. Idolatry. Blasphemy. Murder. Adultery."

John saw that Miss Wallace, the schoolteacher, sat on her hay bale and wept until the front of her bodice was wet with tears. Colin Pritchard and Jeremiah Frost never quite met John's gaze and fidgeted with their hats in their laps. Annie Gray smiled in encouragement.

The girl from the river stood at the back of the schoolyard, holding on to her abdomen with both hands as though suffering from stomach cramps.

As John prepared to deliver the final warning to his flock, he stretched out his arm and pointed at each of the men and women in turn as he made eye contact until . . . he found himself pointing at the vile man the townsfolk called Caswell who leaned against the old oak tree at the rear of the schoolyard.

No one was more shocked than John when a bolt of lightning lit up the town and struck the tree with an earth-shaking explosion.

The panic-stricken crowd scattered, leaving John standing alone, still pointing. Caswell lay crumpled on the ground.

Tiny wisps of smoke rose from scorched leaves. A flame flared in the smallest twigs, then died as a drenching rain began to fall. Around the tree from top to bottom wound the charred path the lightning had traveled.

I did that, John thought.

He lowered his arm and straightened his shoulders. Feeling as powerful as any human could feel, he ran through the rain to Caswell's side. A few men ventured back to the schoolyard to help, but stopped a fair distance from John and stared as though afraid to draw too near.

"Help me lift him," John demanded. "We must get him out of the rain. Into the school?"

The men whispered among themselves, then Jeremiah Frost said, "His mother's cabin."

"It's near?"

"Near enough. We don't want him in the school."

Four men stepped forward to carry Caswell, leaving John to follow.

He walked alone. The men who followed him hung back and talked softly, so only a quiet buzz of voices reached John's ear. He bowed his head in prayer. He prayed for guidance so he could better follow God's bidding, and he prayed for godliness to better save Caswell's soul.

Inside Mary Proud's cabin, as he knelt beside Caswell's bed, John prayed he be given the power to heal. Soon enough, however, he changed his prayer, urging God to hasten the doctor's arrival. Caswell began to thrash around on the bed, shrinking away from John as though he feared another flash of lightning. Caswell's mind might be even more damaged than his body.

Had John indeed brought this horror down on Caswell Proud and his family?

John thrust the thought away as he struggled to calm the injured man, though it seemed he only succeeded in increasing Caswell's panic. When the injured man vomited, John scrambled to his feet and backed away.

Even being inside Mary Proud's cabin for an hour tested John's patience and his dedication to his calling. It wasn't only the nature of Caswell and his mother that disturbed him.

The filth. Dried clods of mud littered the floor around the door. The table was covered with food scraps, some fresh enough to attract flies. John wiped his hands on his pant legs.

The paucity of furnishings, and mean ones at that. Two legs of the wooden table were askew, tilting the tabletop and threatening collapse. Worn bedding lay in wadded mounds on the rickety bed frames. A pile of rags and blankets occupied the corner by the fireplace. A tarnished, dented pot coated with dried food bits hung on the hob.

John chastised himself. He was judging what he did not understand and had not experienced for himself. He bowed his head and prayed that the poor wretched souls who lived in such degradation might be moved to embrace the Lord and thereby improve their lot in life.

He turned toward the door, then stopped when he saw a girl

across the room. Even in the dim light of the partially shuttered cabin, he knew she was the same girl he'd seen at the river. Then, however, she'd appeared winsome and a little mysterious, a part of the wilderness, a water nymph. Now, her dirty bare feet, her tangled and matted hair, and her belligerent stare seemed primitive, even animal-like. John's curiosity was piqued. He walked slowly toward her, afraid of moving too fast for fear she'd run away.

The child held her ground and met his gaze. "Did you kill him?"

Startled by what appeared to be a hopeful expression on the child's face, John said, "No, no. He's alive. The doctor should be here soon."

"Oh."

"What's your name?" he asked.

"Jo Mae. What's yours?"

"Brother John Claymore."

Jo Mae laughed. "You aren't anybody's brother around here. And that's way too long a name for saying when you want to give a howdy to a man. I'm going to call you Preacher."

"You aren't calling him anything of the kind, Jo Mae. And for heaven's sake, this man did not strike your brother down. I'm sorry about Jo Mae," the woman simpered as she attempted to worm her way between John and the cabin door. "She's a rude child, hard to control. A bit fanciful as well. Perhaps you could provide advice? If you would sit down and talk with me for a while—"

"I fear I would be of no assistance. On the subject of young girls, I am most ignorant."

"What about Caswell then? Am I not to receive your compassion, your guidance? Without my son's help, we may very well starve to death."

"The townsfolk will not let that happen, Mrs. Proud. I know

Miss Gray will help you. You needn't worry. But perhaps you could do more for yourself? Find work? This time of the year, there's bound to be farm work, selling products by the roadside, picking beans—"

"I'm not able to do farm work. I'm not strong. I have headaches."

"The Lord helps those—"

"I know, I know. I am quite skilled with a needle, but the headaches . . ."

"Goodbye, Mrs. Proud. I'll pray for you and your family."

The men who lingered outside stepped back, allowing John to pass. As he strode away, he heard Caswell's mother call after him, "Fat lot of good that'll do. You can't eat prayers or burn them for firewood. Worth about as much as a daydream."

He glanced back toward the cabin. The men were still watching him.

John checked the sky. The rogue cloud had moved on. He returned to the schoolyard but found it already cleared of the benches, barrels, and planks. A group of nearly thirty men, women, and children bustled in and out of the schoolhouse. Miss Gray waited in front and beckoned him to join them.

"We have refreshments," she said. "We'll not ask for any more sermonizing, but if you would be so kind, would you lead us in a prayer?"

As drained as he was, both physically and mentally, John still responded when he felt the Lord push him toward the schoolhouse, stand at his side when John bowed his head, and speak through John's mouth with words of hope and love. After he'd said, "Amen," he ate, although later he could not remember what had been on the plate Miss Gray placed before him. He did remember that no one besides Miss Gray approached him to ask his blessing or compliment him on his sermon.

When John finished eating, he gathered his saddlebags and

returned to the blacksmith's cabin, where he slept in a bunk-room attached to the barn. He could hardly stay awake long enough to take off his boots.

Shortly before daybreak, he woke from a nightmare in which dark creatures crawled out from under rocks, and lightning strikes turned the evil-looking things into charred black lumps. Something bumped against the outside wall by his bed. John crept to the door with his blanket wrapped around his shoulders, stepped outside, and peered around the corner of the cabin. He saw nothing in the smithy's yard.

After latching the door, he returned to his bed. Thoughts intruded, preventing sleep. Small ones at first. He tried to remember what he'd eaten at the schoolhouse that might have upset his stomach. He speculated about the bumping noises he'd heard. He wondered what had happened to the little girl.

Then the nightmare returned, jumping into the gentle meanderings of his mind as though it intended to rip his attention away from anything in which it did not play a part. John again saw the shadowy movements, the lightning. He struggled to push the picture away, but only succeeded in enlarging his view. Rocks were everywhere—fields full of them. The dark creatures drifted slowly across the land, floating toward the source of the lightning. John strained to see more clearly. He couldn't make out shapes, couldn't define features. Were they animals? Were they men?

Bolts of lightning rained down toward the rocks, but the figures kept coming. They climbed toward a shining form at the top of a hill, moving like the ocean's tide up the shore. John focused on the light, the source of the lightning. He drifted closer, closer.

He stood on the hill, had become the source of the light. The tide of writhing forms lapped at the toes of his boots—

John jerked awake and sat up. He threw his blanket aside and shifted his position so his bare feet were on the floor. He bowed his head and gripped the side of the bunk as though he expected it to throw him to the floor if he did not hold on.

The darkness unnerved him. He rose from the bunk and fumbled around the dark room until he found the candle he'd tossed on the table. Embers still glowed within the charred logs in the fireplace. He plunged the candle into the hot spot and held it there until the wick flared. He carried the candle back to the table and sat down in the rickety chair. With the light in his right hand, he pulled the bible out of his saddlebag and placed it on the table before him.

With his left hand flat on the front of the book, John bowed his head and prayed for a sign.

He pulled the bible nearer, closed his eyes, and thumbed the pages from the back until he suddenly flipped the book open and placed his hand in the center. Then, eyes still closed, John ran his hand back and forth over the open pages, stopped, and pressed his finger down.

He opened his eyes and leaned forward. *Proverbs*, he thought. *Yes, I thought it would be Proverbs.*

He moved his finger aside and read, "Pride goeth before destruction, and an haughty spirit before a fall."

What did it mean? Was it his destruction that was threatened? His fall? What had he done wrong?

Bewildered, he thought back over the day. Saw the little girl at the river. Entered Sangamon. Saw Caswell and sensed his wickedness. The bible meeting, and the way the Lord had lifted him up and let him shine. Then the lightning bolt and Caswell Proud falling to the ground.

And John remembered his own thoughts at that moment: *I did that.* Those were the words he'd spoken to himself. He was ashamed.

He pushed his chair back and knelt on the floor. Holding the candle above his head with both hands, John prayed. This time, he prayed for humility. He prayed for compassion. He prayed for forgiveness. He prayed until his arms shook with pain, but he kept on praying until the melted wax extinguished the flame.

The backs of his hands burned from the hot wax that had spilled. His shoulders ached with such intensity, he could barely dress himself. That was his penance, one he could tolerate as long as the Lord deemed necessary.

With his arrogance and conceit, had he jeopardized his relationship with the Almighty?

The next morning, John traveled west from the Village of Sangamon until he reached the first fork in the road leading north to New Salem. He needed his father's counsel as he contemplated his future in the ministry.

To push away the niggling memories of his frightening nightmares, John called on more agreeable thoughts of Sangamon. The kind and gentle Annie Gray was first in his mind. He'd meant to talk to her before he left, to ask her what she knew of Caswell Proud's sister. The child was obviously neglected. Most likely unloved. And perhaps mistreated.

Miss Gray is a good, God-fearing woman, he thought. *Hardworking, that's clear.*

She'd never been married, or so he'd been told by at least three Sangamon housewives bent on matchmaking.

I must make it a point to speak to Miss Gray when . . . if I return.

CHAPTER SIXTEEN:
JO MAE LEAVES HOME

Caswell did not talk or get out of bed for days after the preacher raised his arm and let loose the storm on him, and he did not remember anything except the flash of light, and he always said the preacher did it. Caswell got scared of the preacher for a time, and when Mama told him the preacher came to the cabin and prayed over him, Caswell got to shaking like goblins were after him.

When Mama quit telling him about the praying like it was something good, he forgot all about it, but sometimes I'd think about sneaking up on Caswell and yelling, "Preacher's coming," just to see what he'd do. I never did it, though. I think Caswell got scared about the preacher looking on him while he slept, maybe even touching him, like the preacher might put a bad spell on him. I reckon Caswell was scared that he could not run fast enough to get away if the preacher came after him.

After Caswell got better, he started saying words we could figure out, and he'd eat everything Mama'd give him. But when he tried to stand up, it was like watching an old rag doll. He'd fall down and jerk about on the floor like a fish flopping around on dry land, and it took both me and Mama to get him back up on the bed again. Caswell did not remember that, either, but he remembered for sure that I was going to birth a child, and he could not get anything in trade for taking me down by the stable. He'd think about that and get red in the face, and his eyes would get big, and he'd grab his head and pull at his hair and fall back on the bed and yell. He would not stop until I ran out the door so he could not see me.

It was near a month before Caswell got up and walked out the door without falling down, and it was another month before he got past the tree that grew out by the road.

But the better Caswell got at walking, the meaner he got around me. And he acted strange besides, with a lot of twitching and blinking for no reason.

The bad pains in his head did not go away. Mama and me always knew when it happened because he'd get to howling and clawing at his eyes. I watched him and wished one of those pains would make him fall over dead.

But he did not fall over dead. Instead, he started following people around town and getting them all upset with his slobbering and whining, and at night he'd go sneaking around folks' houses. One time I even saw him peeking in the schoolteacher's window, but she saw him doing it and threw a bucket of kitchen slop right out the window, all over his head.

I tried to tell Mama what Caswell was doing out there in the dark, but she never listened. Caswell got so mad at me telling Mama, he tried to catch me, and I figured he was going to punch me hard. He never caught me in the daytime, though, because he ran like a horse with a broken leg and I always got away.

Then Caswell snuck up and grabbed me while I was sleeping. The first time, he punched me hard on the ear and that woke me up right quick, so I scooted away and yelled until Mama woke up and made Caswell go to bed. The second time he got hold of me was real bad, because he was holding on to my arm with one hand and pounding on my face with his fist. I screamed so loud I scared Mama to death, which made her yank me out of bed and send me flying across the room.

I could not stay there with Caswell and Mama anymore.

Neither one cared much whether I was dead or alive. And they sure did not give one hoot for my unborn baby.

CHAPTER SEVENTEEN:
ANNIE DOES HER BEST

One frosty October morning Annie looked out her window to see who knocked at her door. It was Jo Mae, now a thin gangly girl of thirteen with expressive eyes and a solemn demeanor. Annie stared at her for a minute and knew the girl was pregnant, even before she dropped her gaze to Jo Mae's waist and confirmed the roundness of the girl's abdomen. Jo Mae brought her hands up to cover her stomach.

"Miz Gray, you said I could come to you if I ever needed help, and I guess I need more help now than I ever needed before."

Annie said nothing. She opened her door and stood aside to let Jo Mae in. Had the child been violated? Did she indulge in wanton behavior? Her mouth dry and her breath short, Annie wondered these things and what she should say and do. If this child was now tainted by sin, could Annie help her without walking in the shadow of Satan? Would she risk her own good reputation?

Jo Mae's chin lifted and her lips trembled, as though she sensed Annie's reluctance. "I'm going to have a child, Miz Gray, and I am not going to tell you anything about why this happened to me, but I have to get away from Caswell because he's beating on me again, and Mama will not do anything to stop him. They call me hateful names, and you know I cannot bring a little baby into that house and let them treat it like they've been treating me. It's not right."

In spite of her defiant stance and fierce tone, Jo Mae trembled as she asked for help.

Taking pity on the child, Annie sat Jo Mae down in the rocking chair, covered her legs with a quilt, and pulled the kettle to the front of the cast-iron cook stove where it would quickly reach boiling.

"I'll make tea." She patted the girl's shoulder and smoothed her hair.

Annie took a deep breath, started to ask Jo Mae if Caswell had made her pregnant, then changed her mind and did not say anything. She would always wonder, but if she knew for sure, wouldn't she feel compelled to take action? Annie shook her head at her own cowardice, but held her tongue. For the time being.

Over cups of tea and biscuits slathered with apple butter, Annie told Jo Mae what it would be like to carry and bear a baby and how much responsibility it would be. She hesitated, thought of mentioning bitter herbs rumored to end pregnancies, but decided not to speak of them until she learned more. No telling how such things might affect a girl so young.

"I could help you, child, but not if you live with your mother and Caswell. It would be better if you stayed here with me."

Annie paused. Her first thought was to keep the baby and raise it herself. There seemed little chance she would ever marry and have children of her own. But could she do that if there was any chance the baby's father was Caswell Proud?

"You could leave the baby with me for a while, until you're older," she offered, instead.

"No, thank you just the same. I'm this baby's mama." Jo Mae stood up, letting the quilt fall to the floor. She placed her cup on the table and walked toward the door. "And I can't live here with you, Miz Gray, because Caswell would go even crazier than he already is. He'd be sneaking over here and bringing all kinds of trouble."

"Wait, Jo Mae. I have another idea. I know a family of farmers, the Hobarts. They live about thirty miles north of here. Mrs. Hobart needs help with her children. Let me talk to them. Maybe they'll let you stay there until your baby's born. You can earn your keep. I'll talk to the preacher, too. He might know someone in another town who'd be willing to take you and your baby in."

Jo Mae stopped and turned back, hesitated, then said, "You can talk to those farm folks. You tell them I'll work as hard as I can, as long as I can. And I'll be a good mama, Miz Gray. I promise you that."

"Do you want to stay here until I talk to the Hobarts?"

"I'm going back to Mama. I'm supposed to beg Mr. Frost for food."

"Take the rest of the biscuits, Jo Mae. And that head of cabbage. Will that help?"

"Can't, thank you kindly. Mama would know I was here. Has to be something with store-bought wrapping."

Annie had felt a responsibility toward Jo Mae from the moment she was born. She always felt that way about the babies she delivered, especially the girls. Even though Jo Mae's birth had been easy, her life would be hard. The first strike against the child was being female. The second was being an unwanted child in an unhappy house. The third was being the sister of that nasty little boy, Caswell Proud.

For weeks after Jo Mae was born, Annie had visited the family daily, offering late summer produce from her garden, cleaning, and caring for the children.

Mary would say, "I'm so glad you're here. Jo Mae cried all night, and she wouldn't nurse until dawn. Now Caswell is clamoring to be fed, but I'm exhausted. Could you take care of him?"

Of course, Annie always could.

Annie didn't break free from the burden of Mary's exhaustion, headaches, and troublesome children until Jo Mae was nearly five years old. By then, Annie chose to distance herself from Caswell, a rebellious and hostile eleven-year-old, as well as his mother, who continued to take advantage of Annie's good nature.

Annie maintained her satisfying relationship with Jo Mae for another year by encouraging the child to walk the quarter mile to her farm whenever possible.

Jo Mae always stood at the edge of the road and called out her greeting, no matter where Annie was working at the time. "Hey, Miz Gray." If she didn't get an answer, she'd yell again, a little louder.

If Annie labored outside, she'd glance up, and then stand, straightening her back to relieve the ache from bending over her hoe so long. "Hello, Jo Mae," she'd say. "How're you today?"

"Oh, I'm fine," Jo Mae always replied.

One day she said, "Oh, I'm fine, but Mama's getting one of her headaches because she says I'm talking too much and being hateful about Caswell pinching me and pushing me down. Miz Gray, he is so mean, and she will not listen. Now she says I should talk to you because maybe you have chores for me, so do you?"

Annie had sighed and studied the six-year-old. Jo Mae's dress was too small, and the worn fabric needed patching in several places. Her hair was a tangled mess. Mary obviously never used her silver brush on Jo Mae's mop, or even washed the girl's hair for that matter. From the appearance of her filthy arms and bare feet, Jo Mae most likely had not had a bath since the last time Annie had taken the child in hand.

When was that? Annie couldn't remember.

"Chores. Hmmm. Yes, I know just the thing. You'll get dirty, though. Do you mind?"

Jo Mae held out her hands and grinned. "See, Miz Gray? It doesn't matter. My hands are already dirty as can be."

"Good. You can help me spread straw in that stinky old pigpen. After that we'll be a terrible mess. We'll clean you up before you go home."

Later, when Jo Mae stepped into Annie's big washtub, the black and blue marks covering the backs of her arms and thighs were exposed.

Annie gasped. "Child, where did you get those bruises?"

"Caswell did it. He's mean. I'm going to beat on his head with a stick when I get bigger."

"But your mother—"

"She will not listen, Miz Gray. She says I give her a headache because I complain too much. I tell her too much bad stuff about Caswell, and so she gets a headache so she does not have to hear me talking."

"Then, why don't you tell me. Perhaps I'll have a word with your brother."

"You better not, Miz Gray. Caswell's awful bad. And he hurts things. If you talk hard to him, he might do something wicked."

"Like what, dear?"

"Well . . . he told me he's the one who hurt that old dog that lives with the Indian. And he's got the dog's foot. Honest, Miz Gray, I've seen it. He could hurt your pig like that, or your mule, if he had a mind to."

"Did he tell you about the dog in order to scare you?"

"I reckon so. But I'm going to get him back when I get big, Miz Gray. I will not be scared then."

I suspect he'll make sure you're always afraid, child, Annie

116

thought. Aloud she said, "Here's a cloth and soap. You wash up, and then I'll scrub your back and your hair. Mind, you get those feet clean now."

Jo Mae giggled. "I sure do not know what for, Miz Gray. I do not wear shoes, and my feet are going to get dirty again when I walk home."

Annie smiled. She picked up Jo Mae's worn dress and placed it out of sight where she could wash and patch it later. She reached into the cupboard where she stored the printed feed sacks and pulled out the one she used as a pattern for her work shirts. It would have to do for now, even though it was much too large for Jo Mae's thin body.

When Jo Mae was clean, smelling like Annie's lye soap, she let Annie towel her dry and pull the feed sack dress over her head. Jo Mae smoothed the dress with her hands and admired the tiny brown flowers printed on the yellow background.

"This is pretty," sighed Jo Mae. "It's the prettiest dress I ever had."

"And you are lovely in it. Here, let me get the tangles out of your hair. Sit down on the stool. I'll try not to hurt you."

With the child turned away from her, Annie shook her head in dismay. There was so little she could do to help. For now, she wouldn't speak to Mary or Caswell, but would try to keep an eye on the little girl.

"Remember, child, you come to me whenever you need help."

Jo Mae winced at the extra pull on her hair. After that, she sat quietly without complaining until Annie had brushed, braided, and tied her hair with tiny bows made from scraps that matched the feed sack dress. As she left Annie's farm to return home, Jo Mae marched proudly away, turning once to wave at Annie and to display the bottoms of her feet that were already black from the dirt road.

After that day, Jo Mae's visits to Annie's farm abruptly ended.

The child was rarely present when Annie dropped off her baskets of food. Several weeks later, as Annie approached Mary Proud's cabin, she saw Jo Mae running up the street from the store, carrying a small package in her hand.

"Mama's got a headache, Miz Gray. Do not knock at the door or she'll get powerful mad."

"I brought you this—"

"Oh, thank you, but I got to go in and give the medicine to Mama."

"Jo Mae, come back out here for a minute when you're done. I want to talk to you."

"Okay," she said as she slipped inside with the basket and her mother's medicine.

Annie waited. Finally, Jo Mae dashed out the door with a bucket as if she were going to run right past.

"Wait." Annie reached out and grabbed Jo Mae's arm. "I haven't seen you for weeks. Is there anything I can do for you?"

"No, Miz Gray. I'm fine."

Annie lowered her voice to a whisper. "What about Caswell? Is he still being mean to you?"

"He's like always, Miz Gray. I run away from him when I can."

"You can come to the farm and talk to me. Maybe I can help."

"No . . . Mama does not want me to come to your place ever again."

"But I thought she wanted you to come to my farm and do chores."

"Miz Gray, Mama said I should always mind my manners and all, but that you were teaching me to be prissy and put on airs with the ribbons in my hair and the pretty dress, and she said I should never have been taking off my clothes and getting new ones from you, and—"

"Jo Mae, I'm so sorry. But you could work in the garden, couldn't you?"

"Honest, Miz Gray, I can't. I thank you kindly for the carrots and greens, and Mama will be thankful when she's better, but I have to go now. Mama said the barrel's empty and I got to fetch water from the spring."

Jo Mae had run down the street, her long hair flying around her face as the breeze picked up. Annie wondered if Jo Mae had managed to find and use her mother's hairbrush while Mary slept.

Eventually Annie reduced the number of her visits to Mary, restricting herself to an occasional act of charity. She could no longer put up with Caswell's impudent stare, especially with all she knew about him. That Mary remained oblivious to Jo Mae's isolation and misery was intolerable. And it hurt Annie deeply to know that Jo Mae suffered such cruelty but would not accept help.

Now, nearly seven years since she'd last dealt with Mary's family in more than a superficial way, Annie was drawn back into Jo Mae's life. She made preparations for the long ride she would take the next day when she would beg the Hobart family to harbor Jo Mae until the end of her pregnancy.

Chapter Eighteen:
Jo Mae at the Hobart Farm

By the time I had to go begging Miz Gray for help, I had not been to her house for a long time, ever since Mama got mad at me, saying I was begging for pretty things and that the Prouds earned their way in the world. She said we were not taking any more charity from the likes of Annie Gray. I did not understand, because Mama kept on taking whatever Miz Gray brought over in her basket.

Mama and Caswell did not care whether or not I had a nice dress, or if I'd get a ribbon in my hair after I'd washed it with Miz Gray's homemade lye soap that made it smell funny until Miz Gray rinsed it with her rose water. I reckoned Mama did not want anybody looking after me better than she did, even if she never even hardly tried. I waited until she fell asleep before I took that fancy brush of hers to my own hair, which I never thought about doing until I was ten years old.

I knew there were girls not much older than me who were married and already had babies. That made me wonder if it ever happened that a girl got the baby first and then got married. Or was I the only girl who did this bad thing? And maybe no man would want to marry me ever. And then I wondered if I would even get to be fourteen or if Caswell would beat me to death first.

Being big with child was going to make it hard to run away from Caswell when he had one of his temper fits. He'd turned even more hateful since the lightning struck him down and made him crippled—and crazy to boot. And I reckoned Mama was not ever going to stop Caswell from beating on me whenever he wanted, even if she was standing right there in the same cabin and pretending like she was thinking about something else.

Caswell hung around the cabin a lot at mealtime, but he hardly ever slept in the house, even if he did have his very own bed. I do not know if that was because he and Mama stopped getting along after the lightning made him act so stupid, or if it was because he stunk so bad—like sweat and saddle soap and straw dirtied up in a pile of horse manure. I reckoned that Mama had made him get a job in the horse stables, but I never said anything about the smell. I was afraid if I did say something, it might get Mama thinking he ought to be back home.

After Mama started yelling at me about having a baby, and calling me terrible names, I could not think of anything else to do but pay a visit to Miz Annie Gray. She was the midwife for babies in Sangamon and parts surrounding, and she'd been good to me and to Mama, until she got sideways of Mama's bad feelings.

When I went to Miz Gray and asked for help, I did not think for a minute that she'd pay mind to Mama's words. And sure enough, she got busy and talked to some folks she knows, and pretty quick she'd found me the Hobarts who lived on a farm and said they'd give me a bed in the back pantry and three good meals every day until my baby was born. I had to help with the kitchen work, tend to the chickens, and take care of a whole passel of kids.

Just crawling into a real bed, even if it was in a mighty cold room with preserves on the shelves and meat hanging from the rafters, would be like being in heaven. I was used to tucking blankets around myself and curling up in front of the fireplace with a wad of old clothes under my head. Mama got the only real pillow we had—the one stuffed with soft neck feathers from plucked chickens.

The warm November day Miz Gray put me in her little wagon and sweet-talked that old mule to pull us all the way out to the Hobart farm, which took us almost all day long, well, I felt like I was getting born all over again. It seemed like my baby and me might be free of Caswell and Mama forever. We left in the early morning when the gray fog sat right on the top of the river. As we moseyed along to the north, we saw the sun come shining through the fuzzy sky until it busted out like it was going to turn everything yellow. It really did feel like it changed my life and my feelings, maybe even down to the middle of my heart.

When I started listening to Miz Gray again instead of daydreaming about my future life, she told me she thought I was about six months along. That would mean my baby should get born in February, right in the middle of winter. Sangamon Valley had a lot of mighty fierce weather in January and February, sometimes March, too. I wiggled my shoulders like it did not matter. I'd be warm and cozy on the Hobart farm, at least until my baby came. And Miz Gray said she'd find a home for me and my baby so we'd never have to go back to Sangamon. Not ever!

Mr. Hubert Hobart was a big man and looked like he had the strength of ten mules. I was surely going to feel safe while he was around. Even if Caswell ever did find out where I went, he would not get anywhere near me if that Mr. Hobart guarded the door.

Miz Hobart was a bit plump and kind of loud, and she laughed and hugged us like she was happy we were there. And I guess she was happy to see me, because not five minutes after

Miz Gray had climbed in her wagon and got her mule headed to home, Miz Hobart bustled around, told me to peel the potatoes, sent me to the pantry to fetch onions, and even made me empty the chamber pots that had sat under the beds all day long.

She looked to be as strong as Mr. Hobart, and she told me later she worked right alongside of him in the fields and the barn, fixed all those big meals, and then turned right around and took care of her garden and did the curing and canning and preserving. I did not know how she ever found the time to birth all those kids, or keep watch on what they were doing.

There were so many of them, all scurrying around, doing chores, tussling in the barnyard, and making messes everywhere. It took me the first three days I was there to count them and remember all their names and ages. Once I got it straight and learned there were four boys and three girls, and that Maybelle was the oldest and the boy twins, Zeke and Zack, were the youngest, I figured out the rest.

I was happy to find out that Maybelle was almost twelve. I thought maybe we could be friends, which is something I've never had except for Miz Gray, who's lots older than me, but Miz Hobart set me straight real quick. Maybelle was smart and was getting an education and learning how to behave proper so that she could go to a young lady's school in St. Louis. Miz Hobart said Maybelle was not allowed to dawdle with me and learn any of my wild ways, so I was supposed to leave her be, leave her to her chores and her book learning.

I felt ashamed of my life after Miz Hobart told me all that, like I was too dirty and bad to talk to her fancy girl. What was even meaner was the way she told me to clean up after all those children, scrubbing their dirtied britches and all, but not to tell them any stories for fun, especially any stories about me.

I found out real quick I was not good enough to touch Miz

Hobart's nice belongings, either. She had this big wood thing she called a loom, for making fine goods, and when I touched the weaving piece she said was a shuttle, I thought sure she was going to slap my hand away, but she did not.

If Miz Gray had not been so far away, near thirty miles she'd said, I would have marched right out there on that road and walked back to Sangamon. But then I remembered about the cozy bed in the pantry, and thought about what kind of life my baby would have if we lived with Mama, and I decided to stay on the Hobart farm and work hard and keep my thinking to myself.

Only a few days after I got to the farm, Miz Hobart took the horse and wagon and went to Sangamon for supplies, hauling two old breeding sows for trade. I stayed at the house to watch the children, like I was told. Soon as the dust settled from that wagon, Mr. Hubert Hobart walked in the front door and told me I had to help him down in the barn.

I set Maybelle to watching the little ones, and I followed him, all ready to do whatever chore he wanted done, and when he told me to reach over and fetch his glove out of the feed trough, I did it. The next thing that happened, Mr. Hubert Hobart had one hand up under my dress and the other hand pulling at the straps of his overalls, and he had the same look in his eyes that the blacksmith had when Caswell dragged me to the stables right there on the edge of Sangamon. I knew it was no use yelling back then, and there was no sense in yelling now. Only those little children were anywhere close enough to hear.

But this time, there was no Caswell making me do something I did not want to do.

Scrambling and rolling to get away, I got to the wall and pulled myself up off the floor with a rope that hung on a nail next to a shovel and a pitchfork. Looking at that pitchfork got me to thinking about killing Mr. Hubert Hobart.

But then I saw Miz Hobart and all those little ones in my mind, and I grabbed the shovel instead. I turned around and whacked Mr. Hobart right in his big belly, and down he went. He smacked his face into the feed trough and blood went flying everywhere.

Of course, there was nothing I could do but wrap up that man's head with his own shirt, and not knowing for sure if he was alive or dead gave me a bad feeling, but I hung the shovel up on a nail and went up to the house to check on the children. When I went back to see if Mr. Hobart had moved any, I found him sitting up, leaning against the trough.

"What happened?" he asked. He sounded all mixed up and stared at his hand, which got covered with blood when he touched his face.

"You fell down, like you were having a fit or something," I said. I stayed quiet about him touching me, in case maybe he did not remember it anyway.

"A fit? What kind of fit?"

"Well, you reached out like you needed help and then you fell down."

"Oh." Mr. Hobart studied on that fact, then looked up at me like he recollected more than I told him.

"It's lucky that you only hit your head on the trough," I said real slow, thinking he'd figure out what I was telling him and ponder on it.

"Why is that lucky?" he asked as he touched his bloody head again.

"Because, Mr. Hubert Hobart, you came close to knocking that pitchfork right off the wall, and what if you were to fall on a pitchfork? Even as big as you are, those sharp things would go right on through to the other side and you would be dead."

He looked into my eyes, and then when he saw what I was telling him, he stopped looking at me like he was stupid and hung his head so his chin sat on his chest. "Go on back to the house," he said. "Tell Miz Hobart to come help me when she gets home."

"Yes sir, Mr. Hobart," I said, and then I turned and ran back up to the house where I found all those children, including Maybelle, drawing pictures in a big sticky mess of apple butter they had spilled on the table.

While I cleaned up, I thought about Mr. Hobart and wondered if maybe all men had a certain kind of evil in their hearts. I wondered if the preacher knew about this, or maybe if even the preacher had this streak of badness inside himself, but that was something I did not want to think about. There had to be some people who were truly good inside and out, even if they were men.

When Miz Hobart came home and got Mr. Hobart inside the house and stretched out on his bed, she came to ask me what I was doing in the barn. She looked at me in a funny way when I said how Mr. Hobart needed help but then had that fit and fell over. Then she let it be and sent me outside to pick up wormy, spoiled apples off the ground and tote them to the pigpen, which was a hard chore she'd never made me do before that day.

Later on that evening, Miz Hobart told me she was going to get a hired man until Mr. Hobart was back on his feet, and that this hired man would need the bed in the pantry, so she would take me back to Miz Gray in Sangamon the very next day.

I wondered how come my life never turned out the way I thought it ought to, no matter how hard I worked, no matter what words I said to that God that was supposed to be watching over me, and no matter how hard I wished for one of the miracles that's in the bible. And I sure was not going to get a happy life on the Hobart farm, no matter how nice Miz Gray said it would be.

I thought a long time about what I could do. I surely could not go back to Mama's house for even one minute, and I knew Caswell would never let me stay with Miz Gray if Mama did not want me to. So after Miz Hobart and all those children fell asleep, I took my little bundle of clothes and one pair of Miz Hobart's boots, which I know was stealing, but I needed those boots bad. I snuck out the door and down the steps, and I started walking.

It took me a long time to get to the Sangamon River, almost four days, even with part of one day riding on the back edge of a hay wagon that was carrying food to some cows out on the prairie. A boy about as old as Caswell gave me the ride, but he did not talk much and he was not mean.

When I got close to Sangamon, I followed the path deep into the woods, and when I saw Fish's Indian house by the river, I walked right up to the door and waited for Fish to see me and let me in.

Chapter Nineteen:
Fish Shelters the Runaway Girl

When a shadow blocked the sun streaming through his open doorway, Fish glanced at the dog. It lay stretched out nearby, sleeping.

Fish moved his right hand toward his waist where his hunting knife rested in its deerskin sheath. He crept to the doorway and peered outside. There, just to the left of his *wikiyapi,* stood Jo Mae. She waited, as he'd once told her was proper behavior in the Kickapoo tribe, for him to speak.

"Ay, Jo Mae. I have not seen you for many weeks now." He motioned her to come in.

Jo Mae entered, dropped her bundle inside the doorway, then walked to one of the fur rugs near the fire hole in the center of the room. She sat with her legs crossed and pulled her cloak over her knees. She rested her hands in her lap. The dog raised its head and flopped its tail on the floor in greeting.

"Jo Mae, are you hungry? Want water, coffee?"

"I'm hungry and thirsty and cold. I walked a long ways, walked part of four days and all night, too. I reckoned I'd freeze to death if I stopped. My feet are hurting bad." Jo Mae pulled off her boots and showed Fish the broken blisters on her toes and heels. Two of the blisters were bleeding.

"Mmm. I have good medicine. First food and medicine. Then you sleep."

She brushed away the tears that ran down her cheeks and said, "Thank you."

After adding dried branches to his cooking fire, Fish moved around his hut, gathering the cooking rack, the large iron skillet he'd received from the blacksmith in trade for a hand-chipped stone blade, and the long-handled fork he'd carved from a birch limb. He dropped a bit of pork fat into the skillet. When it began to sputter, he used his fork to spread the grease around in the pan before adding two eggs. He threw the shells into the fire, then added two thick slices of side meat to the skillet.

Jo Mae leaned forward and sniffed the greasy, mouth-watering aroma as the meat began to sizzle.

The space around the fire grew warmer. Fish removed the blue and tan wool poncho he wore and adjusted his cloth headband so his long gray hair fell behind his shoulders. He wiped his hands on his buckskin britches, leaving a greasy mark on each thigh.

The dog got up and ambled awkwardly toward the fire. He stared at the food in the pan, then sat down near Jo Mae as though taking his rightful place.

"Where'd you get this meat?" she asked.

"From the white man that lives on the big farm on the other side of the water. One day I walked up river and saw many pigs. I traded deer meat for side meat and hocks. Plenty of meat for beans."

Jo Mae's tears were gone, replaced by a smile that touched Fish's heart. *Where has she been?* he wondered. *Why has she walked so far? Why did she come here?*

It wasn't good manners to pry, at least not good Kickapoo manners. Most of the white people he knew would ask personal questions whenever they wanted, especially of a child. Even so, he waited. He had a feeling Jo Mae would tell him everything when she was ready. He smiled to himself, remembering what a talker she had been on previous visits to his camp, even though he understood little of what she rambled on about. She talked fast and used many strange words.

She acted different today. Little talk, many tears. Fish felt her tension as much as he saw it in the rigid set of her jaw and the trembling of her hands. Still, he waited.

He scooped the cooked eggs and meat onto a tin plate, added a wooden spoon, and handed the plate to Jo Mae. He studied her flushed face, now more rounded than the last time he had seen her. She could not have been without food for more than a few days.

Jo Mae saw Fish watching her. She took a deep breath as though about to erupt into a flurry of words, then shook her head. Breaking the last of the crispy meat into two pieces, she ate one and fed the other to the dog.

"Bread?"

"Yes, please." Jo Mae took the hunk of dry cornbread and nibbled at it as she stared into the fire.

"First you put medicine on your feet. Then you sleep."

Jo Mae held her cloak tight around her body as she limped to the pile of rugs in the corner. This was her space, where she'd often rested when she was younger and would come to listen to the stories Fish told her of Kickapoo life in the days before the White Man came.

He helped her apply liniment to her blistered feet and wrap them in soft strips of deerskin. Her hands and feet were cold, as though she'd been playing in the icy river. When she was comfortable, Fish pulled the old bearskin cover off his wooden bed frame and placed it over her. He picked up one of the large warm stones that circled the fire pit and wrapped it in an old buckskin shirt. He placed the stone under the blanket near her feet. She didn't move. She was already asleep.

Fish pulled the tail of his tunic over his hunting knife, threw his poncho over his shoulders, and stepped out into the cold breeze. He sniffed the air and studied the clouds hanging low over the river.

Snow. Or rain that would turn to ice when it touched the tree branches. Too cold for a young girl here.

The dog wandered outside and sniffed the air just as Fish had. It nudged Fish's leg with its nose and accepted Fish's absentminded pat before it went back inside.

Fish leaned through his doorway and took one more look at Jo Mae. She was still sound asleep. The dog had curled up on the cover near the warm stone at the girl's feet. Fish shifted the poncho on his shoulders to cover his neck, tucked his hands into his shirt to warm them, and set off toward the village.

By the time he reached Annie Gray's farm, Fish felt cold to the bone. He wondered how Jo Mae, a small white girl, had survived a walk that must have been long and difficult, if one judged by the many blisters on her feet. At Annie's gate, Fish paused, wondering if he was doing the right thing. He would not go to Jo Mae's mother. She was bad and Caswell was worse. Fish did not know the rest of the villagers very well. Annie Gray was the only one he could trust.

Fish shuffled to her door. It opened before he had a chance to knock.

"Fish, you must be freezing. Come in and get warm."

He hesitated, and then entered. Annie put the kettle over the fire and cleared a pile of rags from a chair.

"Please, Fish, sit down. I'll make tea."

Amazed at having been invited inside Annie Gray's cabin and uncomfortable about broaching the subject of his visit, he sat on the chair and gazed into Annie's fireplace while she bustled about behind him. She talked as she worked, but he caught very little of what she said. She spoke too fast.

Annie filled her flowered teapot with hot water and returned the kettle to the back of the fire. Finally, she poured the tea into two cups covered with little blue flowers. She sat in a chair across from him and picked up her cup. Fish concentrated on holding the teacup, trying to push his finger through the handle. It would not fit. Finally, he gripped the cup with both hands.

Annie said, "What did you bring for trade?"

"Mmm," Fish answered. "I did not come for trade."

"Do you need eggs, or meat? You can bring trade another day."

"No, I'm not here to trade. It's Jo Mae," he explained. "She came to my door. Her feet were bleeding, needed medicine. She was cold and tired. She had walked a long way."

Where has she been? Where is she going? He wanted to ask those questions, but good manners prevented such a direct approach.

Startled, Annie Gray sat up straight and stared at Fish. "When did she come back?"

"This day. I gave her food and medicine for her feet. She's asleep now."

"And she didn't say why she came back?"

"She did not talk. She was sad, cried. I helped Jo Mae, but a woman would help better." Fish shrugged. "Jo Mae did not talk. Maybe she is sick."

"Fish, I'll come see Jo Mae at the river. She should not return to Sangamon. If Caswell found her here, he might hurt her."

Fish sighed. "You will come soon?"

"Yes. It's still early. She's healthy. The baby's not due until spring. She should be fine if you let her spend the next few weeks with you. In the meantime, I'll try to find another place for her to live."

Fish dropped the teacup to the floor. It broke into four pieces, adding to his confusion and embarrassment. As he scrambled to pick up the broken china, he felt his face flush but was unsure whether from shame at showing bad manners in this kind white woman's home, or from the startling information that Jo Mae was going to have a baby. Was that what Annie Gray really meant?

"You say Jo Mae have a baby?" Fish forced himself to ask as he handed the china shards to Annie.

"Yes." Then, as if she realized Jo Mae had not told him, she said, "Fish, I'm so sorry. I thought you already knew. Did you not wonder when you saw her?"

"No. She did not talk. She wore a big coat. She still wore the coat when she went to sleep."

Fish dropped back onto the chair and thought about this new and appalling piece of information. He wanted to know who the father was, feared it might be Jo Mae's brother.

Annie Gray answered his unspoken question. "She won't tell me who the father is."

"Not that boy Caswell." Without pausing to think, Fish placed his hand on the hilt of his hunting knife.

"She says no. Not her brother."

Fish let out the breath he'd been holding. He took his hand away from the knife. He sat quietly, hoping Annie Gray would tell him more.

She waited a moment, then said, "I thought I'd found her a safe place to live, Fish. The Hobart farm. She was to help Mrs. Hobart in return for her bed and meals. I can't imagine what happened."

"She will tell you. You will come soon?" he asked again.

"I'll come tomorrow. Will you still help Jo Mae? Even if she is going to have a baby?"

"Yes. She is only a small girl. This is a bad thing for Jo Mae, but she is not a bad girl. I don't know if my *wikiyapi* is a good home for a small girl and a baby. It is a hard life. What if she gets sick? Or the baby dies?"

"Fish, don't worry. For now, I think Jo Mae is safe with you. I'll help you. I'll make sure you have everything you need. I'll

133

come by often."

"Make sure Caswell does not follow."

Annie's head jerked up at Fish's words. "You've seen him?"

"Yes. Too bad he did not die when the lightning hit the tree. Now he is out at night like a bear with an arrow stuck in its nose. He makes much noise. Even a strong man like an Indian would be afraid of Caswell. He is quiet during the day. He hides in the corner, under a window, behind a door. One day I saw him follow the schoolteacher. When he saw me, he ran like a crazy rabbit with a crooked leg."

Fish stood up and motioned toward the broken cup Annie had placed on the table. He didn't know what to say, but wanted to apologize for the damage he'd done.

Annie waved it away. "It was an old cup, Fish. Most of them have chips and cracks. They break very easily. It doesn't matter."

Fish started toward the door. "I will go now. You come tomorrow. I will tell Jo Mae you come tomorrow?"

"Yes. Tomorrow."

As Fish hurried toward the river, he thought back to the day he'd first seen Jo Mae—the day she was born. He'd known that growing up in a family like hers would be hard.

Even so, taking in a young pregnant white girl was something no male Kickapoo elder would ever consider if he lived with his tribe. If such an unlikely situation had presented itself, the task would have fallen to an older woman, probably one with no family of her own. In such a case, the white girl might be adopted into the tribe, but more likely would have remained an outsider and treated like a servant.

Here Fish was, separated from his tribe by a great distance, ready to take in this girl as if she were his own grandchild. Fish smiled to himself and quickened his pace, eager to return to his camp.

Out of the corner of his eye, he spotted Caswell pressed against the side of the blacksmith shop, watching Fish walk down the street. Fish stopped and glared as he lifted the edge of his poncho and exposed the hilt of his knife.

Caswell turned away and limped toward the stable at the rear of the shop.

Fish followed.

CHAPTER TWENTY:
CASWELL'S FEAR

Caswell was scared of the Injun, even though he couldn't remember why until Fish pulled up his poncho and Caswell saw the knife. He turned quickly and lowered his head, thinking about his steps, trying to stay on the path. He finally glanced over his shoulder and saw Fish on his heels. Caswell's heart pounded. His throat dried up so he couldn't swallow. He tried to take a deep breath but couldn't suck the air in deep enough. Little baby sounds came out of his mouth until he remembered the words and cried out for help.

The Injun dropped his poncho over the knife and walked away.

Caswell's scared feeling left as soon as the Injun disappeared. He was supposed to do something, supposed to go somewhere. He squeezed his eyes closed and tried to remember.

He had a mixed-up way of going places. He stared at one thing and then another instead of looking all around while he walked like other people did. That didn't stop him from thinking about things, but the things he thought about looked like shadows and moved real slow. Besides that, he couldn't hear so well. People yelled, if they talked to him at all. The yelling pushed words at him so fast and hard they got drowned in a big puddle in his head.

It was the preacher's fault. Caswell knew that for a fact. The preacher pointed at him and made a bolt of lightning come flying at his head, leaving nothing behind but an ugly body that might as well be dead.

Dead. Preacher.

Caswell giggled with his mouth hanging open, then wiped the drool from his chin with the back of his hand. His head jerked up as he laughed again.

He stopped. There was nothing in front of him but the open path to the road that followed along the river. Caswell stared as far up the road as he could see. He put his hand to his forehead and pushed until it hurt.

Where?

The places he knew went through his mind one at a time until he saw a picture of the cabin where he lived. Then he saw inside, the rocking chair, Mama. He turned and went back through the village until he got home.

"I'm here, Mama."

There was no answer, but he didn't expect one. He threw his coat on the floor and crept toward his bed. He lay down on his back, his arms stretched wide. His stomach rumbled but he knew he should not ask for food.

Wait. Wait for Mama to say.

He slept, but had no feel for how much time had passed when he woke up. He threw off the quilt, lowered his legs over the side of his bunk, and struggled to sit up. Grabbing his grumbling stomach, he looked around the room. Three potatoes left from Annie Gray's basket sat in plain sight. He got to his feet and checked the rocking chair and then behind the hanging blanket on Mama's side of the room. When he did not see her, he lunged toward the table, grabbed all three potatoes and stuffed two into his pockets. He shoved the third into his mouth as he limped toward the door.

To free up both hands, he bit down on the half-eaten potato and left it sticking out of his mouth. He opened the door, and there stood Mama. Her hands were on her hips, and she gave him an evil eye that would scare the horns off the devil.

Caswell gobbled the potato into his mouth and chewed as fast as he could, afraid Mama would jerk it right out of his mouth. Then he stopped chewing as he figured out what was wrong. His eyes grew big and his mouth dropped open. "You're outside," he said.

"Be quiet, Caswell."

"You been up the road?"

"There's the basket by the door. Pick it up and put it on the table."

"Okay, Mama. What's in the basket?" Caswell reached down to lift off the apron she'd put on top.

Quicker than his eye could follow, Mama slapped his hand. "Don't do that! I told you to take the basket inside. I didn't tell you to inspect it."

Inspect. While he tried to figure out the word, he rubbed the back of his hand.

"Now!" Mama yelled. "Do it now!" She shoved him out of her way as she walked into the cabin. Inside, she glanced at the table, then turned back to Caswell. "Put the basket on the table and get out of here."

"Mama, did you get us vittles?" He stared at the basket, wanting to reach out again and move the apron.

"You already ate."

"What?"

"The potatoes!" she yelled. "You ate the potatoes. I've told you never to eat anything unless you ask me first. Now you go on. Git!"

Caswell reached into his pockets and pulled out the two potatoes he had left, placing them gently on the table. "There, Mama. I only ate one."

"You can go on and eat the other two because that's all you're getting today." Mama grabbed them and tossed them at Caswell's feet.

He picked them up and stuffed them into his pocket. After one last look at the basket, he walked out the door. As he took off down the road, he heard the door slam shut behind him. He pulled one of the potatoes out of his pocket and took a bite. It tasted like flour, but sweet, too. Crunchy. He wondered what Mama had in the basket.

Then he wondered where Jo Mae was. But if he knew where she went, he still wouldn't give her one of his potatoes. And he wouldn't tell her about the basket, either.

For a minute he wished Jo Mae would stay gone forever. Then he thought about how he used to get food and whiskey from men who liked Jo Mae. And how he didn't get so much of those things any longer because Jo Mae was getting a baby.

A bad feeling rose up in his chest and filled his head. It got so big he heard sounds like right after the school bell rang. He tried to run, thinking about the river and how he might make his head better if he stuck it in the water. But the river ran along the other side of town, and it was too cold, and the running wasn't going the way it ought to. He got his feet all tangled up. His arms flapped all over the place. He lost his balance in front of the general store and lay stretched out on the road, staring up at the clouds until Mr. Frost came out and told him to get up and be on his way.

When Caswell stood, he couldn't remember which way he was going before he fell. He went through the pictures again until he reached the one where the old Injun stood in the road. A prickly feeling ran down the back of his neck. He stared in the distance in all directions, but didn't see anyone. He went back to thinking, remembered the basket. He shuffled around until he headed the other direction, and he walked home.

CHAPTER TWENTY-ONE:
MARY'S DESPAIR

Mary was losing control of Caswell. It made her afraid. She had ordered him out the door, but knew he'd be back, demanding more to eat.

She'd talk to him then. Tell him he needed to make himself useful again since he'd lost his job at the stables. Maybe Miss Gray knew where Jo Mae had gone, even though she'd told Mary she had no idea. Truth was, Mary needed Jo Mae to do the things that weren't getting done anymore. Caswell couldn't run errands, and he scared people. They didn't feel sorry for him like they usually did with Jo Mae. Even Miss Gray wouldn't have anything to do with Caswell.

Mary decided she'd tell Caswell to follow Annie around town, see if she'd lead him to Jo Mae. It was his fault Jo Mae had left. He could get busy and get her back home again.

During the years she'd counted on Caswell to provide food for their table and gather hand-me-downs and castoffs for clothing and supplies, Mary had refused to leave her one-room cabin to face the village. When she realized Jo Mae was pregnant, Mary had warned the girl over and over not to tell anyone.

"If people find out," Mary cautioned, "they'll run us out of town." It had been many years since those women had forced her to leave the Fort Dearborn area, but she'd not forgotten how cruel people could be.

"Who fathered this bastard?" Mary had demanded.

"Don't know." Jo Mae got that belligerent expression on her face and glared at Mary.

She gasped. "You've been with more than one boy?"

Jo Mae stared at her without answering.

"Jo Mae? Have you gone deaf and dumb? Answer me."

"Mama, I've told you a hundred times what Caswell's been making me do, and you don't ever listen so I won't tell you anything else. Anyway, they aren't boys, Mama. Those are grown men, and there's a hundred of them so you will never know who this baby's daddy is, not in a hundred years."

Jo Mae's face had gone white except for two bright red spots high on her cheeks. She looked like the precious doll with the painted china head that used to sit propped against a lace-trimmed pillow on Mary's bed in Philadelphia. As always, when she recalled any of her long-gone childhood treasures, she thought of her father and wondered what had happened to him. She had stared past Jo Mae and focused on her own thoughts, forgetting for the moment the new burdens her wayward daughter had deposited on her shoulders.

Jo Mae ran out the door, but Mary did not call her back.

The day of the bible meeting, when Jo Mae had run home from the schoolyard, screaming that Caswell had been struck by lightning, Mary thought the world had come to an end. She stood at the door, her hands covering her mouth as she moaned in anguish and thought, *Caswell's dead!*

His arms hung down and swung back and forth as the men carried him inside and placed him on his bunk. His head lolled to one side. His legs bent awkwardly at the knees. Mary froze, unable to touch her son, to straighten his limbs or place a pillow under his head.

Rustling noises and low murmurs drew Mary's attention toward the door. The preacher worked his way past the men who blocked the doorway. As they saw him pass by, they pulled away.

"Missus, I'm John Claymore. The preacher." He knelt by Caswell's bunk and placed his hand on Caswell's forehead. "Let us pray," the preacher murmured, bowing his head and closing his eyes.

Caswell's eyes popped open, but he didn't move.

The men remaining near the door snatched off their hats and bowed their heads.

Mary, taken aback by the preacher's sudden appearance and the influence he had over the men, almost bowed her head as well. She caught herself, grimaced, and folded her arms across her chest, glaring at the kneeling man who ministered to her son. Still, she did not interrupt his prayer. Instead, she studied his silky hair, which hung almost to his shoulders, the weathered skin on the backs of his hands, his clean fingernails, and his broad shoulders and narrow hips. She glanced up once at a man who stood near the door, perused his bulky midsection and dirty hands, and then returned her gaze to the preacher.

His silent prayer completed, the preacher whispered "Amen," and removed his hand from Caswell's forehead. The white skin where his hand had rested retained a damp pink imprint.

Caswell closed his eyes. His legs twitched. Suddenly he jerked his hand up to cover his mouth, sat up, and vomited into his lap.

Mary looked frantically around the room until she spotted Jo Mae huddled in the corner of Mary's bed. "Get the bucket."

Jo Mae scrambled off the bed and pushed past the men in the doorway to get outside.

The preacher used his linen handkerchief to dab at the splatters on his shirt. Mary hurried to his side and placed her hand on his shoulder. "Come over to the table. I'll help you clean up."

He ignored her.

"Preacher," she said, gripping his shoulder and giving it a little shake.

Caswell grabbed his head with both hands and moaned.

The preacher shrugged off Mary's fingers, stuffed his handkerchief into his back pants pocket, and reached his hands toward Caswell.

"Lie down, Caswell. I'll help you."

As soon as the preacher's hand touched Caswell's shoulder, Caswell's eyes snapped open and his body jerked violently. He cried out and pressed his hands against his temples. His eyes opened wide as he stared at the preacher.

"No!" Caswell screamed. "No, no, no!"

Mary put her hands over her ears.

The preacher drew his hand back as though he'd touched a hot stove. He stood up and backed away.

Jo Mae rushed inside. She carried an empty bucket and shoved it at her mother while she stared at Caswell. "Why's he yelling like that?" she whispered.

Mary grabbed the bucket out of Jo Mae's hand and thrust it under the girl's nose. "Water, Jo Mae. Put water in it."

Jo Mae took the bucket and sighed. "You did not say, Mama." She turned, glanced once more at Caswell, who now babbled without making any sense, and ran outside with the bucket.

"Preacher," said Mary as she tapped him on the shoulder. "Maybe you're the one who's upsetting Caswell. Come over here by the table. If you take off your shirt, I'll get Jo Mae to clean it up."

The preacher turned away from her, took two steps toward the door, then stopped as Jo Mae staggered in, lugging a full bucket of water. She set it on the floor by the side of the bed.

Caswell suddenly paled and grew still.

"Did you kill him?" Jo Mae asked the preacher.

Mary was shocked by the question, but quickly squelched Jo Mae's preposterous notion as she tried to get the preacher's attention and keep him in the cabin.

Jo Mae watched Caswell for a moment, as though preparing to clean him up, but then she backed away. She ran out the door before Mary could object.

"Doc's coming," yelled one of the men standing outside.

The preacher backed away from Mary as he politely fielded her questions. Mary stood by the table with her hands on her hips. The heat rose in her neck. She could tell her pale skin had turned red. She was not sure whether her anger or her humiliation was strongest, for she felt both.

"Get out," she yelled.

The preacher turned to go.

"You're not helping him," she cried. "He needs rest, not all this poking and praying. Go on."

Shortly after the preacher walked out the door, the doctor rushed in and hurried to the bed. Suddenly Caswell began flailing his arms and legs. He kicked the doctor's bag onto the floor and hit him in the nose with his elbow.

"Mrs. Proud, I need your help."

Mary didn't move. Images spun through her mind so fast she felt dizzy. Caswell an invalid. Caswell crippled. Caswell dead. What would she do?

The doctor glared at her. "Right now. You need to hold his head still." He glanced at the men hovering in the doorway. "You, Samuel, hold his legs down. Let's try to keep him from hurting himself."

Caswell struggled but did not open his eyes or speak.

The doctor shook his head and shrugged his shoulders. "I don't know what to tell you except he's lucky to be alive." He handed Mary a small brown bottle. "This is laudanum. It's like opium, strong enough to kill that young child of yours, so keep it hid away so she can't get into it. If you put a couple of drops in a cup of water and get Caswell to drink it, it'll calm him and ease his pain. Give him two more drops if it doesn't work the first time. No more than that until four hours have passed."

Caswell grew still again. His head slumped to the side. He yawned, closed his mouth, and began to snore.

"Is he going to die?"

"I don't know. We'll let him rest now. I'll come back tomorrow. Take care with the medicine. Don't let your little girl get hold of it."

Mary clutched the bottle in her hand as Samuel and the doctor backed away from Caswell's bedside and left her alone with her son.

A few days passed before Mary was convinced Caswell would survive. After a few more days, she understood he would never recover completely, that he would never have the wit or the strength to provide as he had in the past. Jo Mae helped out some, but spent more energy tormenting Caswell and complaining about him than she did trying to help him.

The day Mary lost her temper and slapped Caswell because he'd asked her for food at least twenty times, she realized he'd never be useful again. She had to leave the cabin and assume responsibility for supporting her family, such as it was. Sick and tired of saying she had nothing to give him, Mary grabbed the basket from the bench by the fireplace, dumped dried tomato stems and mouse droppings onto the floor, and walked out the door.

The sun hurt her eyes, but her treasured bonnets had worn out long ago. She'd thrown all of them into the fire when she'd become frustrated at not finding even one with its ribbons still attached. Tears had rolled down her cheeks as she remembered herself young and beautiful. Remembered herself wealthy. Now she didn't even have a sunbonnet made of flour sacking.

Mary squinted and shaded her eyes with her hand as she forced herself on toward Annie Gray's farm. She hated going to the woman for help. Mary preferred Annie stopping by as though making a social call. It seemed less like begging. But now, she didn't know what else to do. She would be even more humiliated if she had to go to the general store and ask for help. Others would hear and see. The word would spread. Her shame would grow.

Before Caswell's accident, Mary had ignored what she didn't want to know. How had he provided for them? If he worked, she didn't know where. She'd never asked. He must have worked for the storekeeper, the blacksmith, maybe farm work. He'd not been gone regular hours, or for long periods of time, but she chose to overlook those things. She assumed Caswell was hard-working and efficient.

When she'd reached the front door of Annie's house, she had hesitated. She was on the verge of sneaking away when Annie walked around from the side of the house, leading a mule by a rope tied around its neck.

"Mary, what are you doing here? Is something wrong?"

Mary burst into tears and dropped her basket on the ground.

Annie tried to rush forward but the mule dug in its heels and refused to move. "Oh, bother! Let me tie him up. You wait here."

By the time Annie returned, Mary had wiped her eyes on her sleeve and regained her composure. She had willed herself to stay and wait by Annie's door.

Once seated by the fire inside the spacious cabin, holding a china teacup full of an aromatic black tea, Mary relaxed. Annie was friendly and she was kind. She prattled on about her farm work and how she'd had little time to make calls on her friends, and what a nice surprise to see Mary up and about and, by the way, she had gathered many more fruits and vegetables than she could preserve, so Mary must take a basket home with her.

"How's your boy doing, Mary? Any improvement? Such a horrible thing to happen."

Mary burst into tears again. "He's never going to get better," she wailed. "He can't walk right. When he talks, he jumbles his words up so they don't make sense. He has terrible headaches, worse than mine. He'll never be able to work again. He tried a job at the stables, but they said he couldn't even muck out the stalls. And *she* provided no help whatsoever. *She* wouldn't even get near Caswell."

"Jo Mae, you mean."

"Yes." Mary wondered how much Annie knew. The woman couldn't have learned of Jo Mae's pregnancy. Mary had stopped Jo Mae from hanging around Annie's house long ago.

"I haven't seen Jo Mae for a long time," Annie said. "Tell her I'll have chores for her if she wants to stop by."

"She won't have time. I need her at home. The reason I came all this way . . . well, with Caswell injured like he is . . . we've no way to get food." She stood and smoothed her skirt, choosing to examine the worn, wrinkled fabric rather than meet Annie's gaze. "I do have to go. Thank you for the tea. If I may, I'll take you up on your kind offer to let us have your extra fruit and vegetables."

"Mary, you and your family need meat as well. And bread."

"That's so generous," Mary whispered.

"As long as Caswell is unable to work, you bring your basket over every week. I'll gladly give you what I can spare."

Mary had taken her at her word.

Every week, Mary walked to Annie Gray's farm and returned with a basket of food, which she then stretched to make last a full week. Caswell lumbered in and out of the cabin all day and had little to think about except his growing appetite. Mary hid things from him, but he'd search the cabin from top to bottom and then start over again.

One day Caswell ate a whole boiled chicken. That was the final straw. Mary whacked him over the head with a hunk of firewood and told him he could not eat anything ever again without her permission. After that, she had to put up with his whiny begging, but it was better than having all the food gone the first day she brought it home.

Then, about the time summer gave way to fall, Jo Mae disappeared without saying one word to Mary. Mary suspected Annie Gray knew more than she said.

"I'm worried about her," Mary had told Annie on one of her weekly visits. "I'm afraid she's lying dead somewhere, maybe in the river."

"Perhaps she ran away. I'm sure she's fine."

"Why would she run away? She had a roof over her head, a warm place to sleep, and enough to eat, thanks to you, Miz Gray."

Mary watched Annie take a deep breath. Then she said, "Jo Mae was terrified of Caswell."

"Oh, I don't think so. Even after getting herself—"

"With child?"

Mary refused to look Annie in the eye. "That's ridiculous. Why would you say that? Caswell . . . oh, you don't think . . . oh, absolutely not."

"Think what?"

Mary grabbed her cloak off the bench by the fire. She threw it around her shoulders, hefted the full basket off Annie's table, and started toward the door. With one look back, Mary smiled as though nothing disturbing had passed between them. "You've been generous as always," she said. "Thank you."

Mary walked briskly away as she considered what Annie had said, and what it might mean.

Chapter Twenty-Two: Annie's Secret

Annie shut the door behind Mary and shook her head with disgust. She thought Mary an accomplished actress, expert at portraying herself as forlorn and lost. But Annie acted her part as well—kind and generous Christian.

In her heart Annie disdained the shameless woman who allowed her son to intimidate townsfolk and mistreat his little sister. And it enraged her to think of Jo Mae, now fourteen-years-old and only months away from delivering a child of her own, a babe who might have been fathered by Caswell himself. This could not have happened if Mary had watched over and protected her daughter.

Now that Jo Mae was safe, it became difficult for Annie to do her Christian duty, if indeed it was her Christian duty, to minister to a common tramp and her son, who may have been spawned by the devil for all she knew.

What's done is done, she thought. She'd keep her promise and give the woman food when she came begging.

When Annie, her hands crusted with curing salt, answered the door several weeks later, she expected to see Mary with her empty basket. Her mouth dropped open in surprise to find John Claymore, the preacher, on her doorstep. She removed her apron and used it to rub her hands clean as she motioned him inside.

"Back so soon?" she asked. "I thought it took near six months to ride your circuit."

"I've sorely neglected my duty to my flock, Miss Annie. After the unfortunate events that occurred here . . . the lightning . . ."

"Yes."

"I traveled to New Salem to stay with my parents. I wanted to consult with my father."

"You're not going to abandon us?"

"Oh, certainly not."

"Goodness, you frightened me. Please, sit down. I'll make tea."

Annie bustled about her stove and cupboards, placing a plate of biscuits on the table along with her finest cups. She glanced at John from time to time, but said nothing.

John stared into the fireplace and continuously jiggled his leg, turned his hat round and round in his hands, and occasionally wiped the palms of his hands on his pants.

Finally Annie spoke. "Is something bothering you?"

"Ah, well, yes."

After a moment, she continued. "You're not here on your regular circuit, so will there be a prayer meeting tonight?"

"I hadn't planned . . . but I suppose—"

"Then why are you here?"

The preacher cleared his throat and stared into Annie's eyes for a moment. He averted his gaze as he blurted, "There are two things I wish to discuss with you."

"And what would the first one be?" Annie felt as though she were pulling her reluctant mule through a patch of thorny bushes.

"The last time I was here, when the lightning . . . I went inside the cabin with Caswell Proud, his mother, and the little girl. I'd seen her before. An unusual child—"

"Yes, she's different from them."

"I'd like to help her."

Annie raised her eyebrows and, for the first time, appraised the preacher as a man instead of a man of God. "Help her in what way?"

"I don't know. I hoped you would advise me. It's clear she is given little care. I suspect she receives no loving embrace from her mother, and must take abuse from her brother."

"You know the girl is with child?"

His face flushed a deep red. "No. How appalling . . . she's only a child herself."

"It's true. I found her a place to stay on a farm far away from Sangamon, but she's come back, I hear."

"To her mother?"

"No. Do you know Fish, the Indian who lives by the river?"

"Yes, but not well."

"Jo Mae turned to Fish for help. He agreed to let her stay with him. She won't come into town because she doesn't want her mother or Caswell to know where she is."

"She's living with the Indian? There's only a shack built of branches and long grass. With the cold and snow . . . won't she be in danger? And with a baby? I don't see how they can live like that."

"Well," Annie said, "the Indians lived like that for a very long time before we came along to show them a better way, and in many places they live like that even today. Fish told me he has blankets and supplies and plenty of food. When he learned of the baby, he assured me he would let me know when I am needed. I'll talk to Jo Mae soon, after she's had time to rest. I want to know why she came back."

The preacher frowned. "But to live there with the Indian . . . those two alone. Does it not seem improper?"

Annie laughed. "You think it important she be proper? For whom would she keep up appearances?"

"I didn't mean . . . it's the heathen. . . ." John shrugged.

"Perhaps it doesn't matter."

"I truly think not."

"Will you tell anyone else? The doctor?"

"No. He cannot keep a secret. Everyone would know. And now that Caswell staggers about like a wild dog who's taken sick, he'd hear talk."

"Is he dangerous?"

"I don't know. He follows me when I go to the store. When I take the mule back to the fields, I see him lurking on the road."

"He is different then, since the lightning?"

"Yes. The injuries he received are clearly permanent. His movements are awkward, his speech garbled. He stares into the distance with his mouth hanging open as though he's forgotten where he was going or what he wanted to do."

John bowed his head.

Annie leaned across the table and patted the preacher's hand. "You're not to blame, John. Caswell Proud was the master of his own fate. He traveled down a path of destruction long before you came to Sangamon." She pulled her hand back and placed it in her lap. "Now, you said there were two things you wanted to talk about."

"Yes." Apparently encouraged by Annie's use of his first name, John rubbed his hands on his pants again, then gripped the tops of his knees. He cleared his throat, opened his mouth, took a breath, closed his mouth, stared at his hands, then took a deeper breath, squared his shoulders . . . and slumped back in his chair.

Annie's first reaction was to smile at the preacher's discomfort, but then she began to feel uncomfortable. Once again, she observed John Claymore as a man instead of a preacher. She bowed her head slightly and began to shake it gently back and forth, aggravated she had not foreseen his intentions.

"No," she whispered.

John sat up straight. "What?"

Annie looked John in the eye. "I fear you are about to ask something of me. If that is so, no matter what it might be, my answer will be no."

She studied his face, intent on making him understand.

John's mouth moved as if he were trying out words he might say in response. Finally, he stood and clutched his hat against his chest with both hands. "I must be going. Thank you for the tea, Miss Annie."

"You won't be staying in Sangamon tonight?"

"It would be best if I continued on. I'll hold services in Sangamon in a few weeks."

John swept through the door, cramming his hat on his head as soon as he was outside. When she called out to wish him a safe journey, he did not answer. He sat ramrod straight on his brown and white pinto as he rode away from her cabin.

Annie put her soiled, wrinkled apron back on and tied the strings at her waist. She returned to the wooden counter she'd built near her fireplace and scooped out a dry layer of salt from the wooden bin by the wall. After pulling the ham onto the gritty surface, she massaged handfuls of salt into the meat.

Later, Annie wrapped her salted cuts of pork in layers of burlap and hung them from the rafters in the coolest corner of the cabin, away from her fireplace. Then she carried two buckets of water inside from her rain barrel. Using a stiff scrub brush and lye soap, Annie scrubbed the salt and meat juices from her arms and hands. After she dumped the first bucket of dirty water into her slop pit, she returned to the cabin and peeled off her homespun work dress.

Using a lavender soap she'd cajoled the grocer into ordering from Boston, and a cloth cut from worn denim pants, Annie bathed in the water from the second bucket. She stood close to the fireplace while she dried herself with the soft towel she'd ordered from the same Boston shop that carried the lavender soap.

She tossed the towel over the chair near the fire, then strode naked into her bedroom. First, Annie brushed her hair until it crackled with energy and reflected the light from her candle. Full of static electricity, her hairs flew around her head as she moved about the room. She lifted the lid of her clothing chest and pulled out clean undergarments and a long-sleeved blue dress with white lace at the neckline, cuffs, and hem. When she was dressed, she added a white handkerchief tucked into one sleeve. She sat on the edge of her bed to pull on the high button shoes she wore for special occasions.

Before she stood up, Annie retrieved a leather sheath containing a hunting knife from under her pillow and attached it to her thigh by tying the leather thongs around her leg. From the hooks on the bedroom wall, she took her blue bonnet and put it on, looping the grogram ribbons under her chin. She lifted down her white woolen shawl and placed it around her shoulders.

As she walked through the main room of the cabin, Annie considered once again how she might secure her cabin from the outside. Now that Caswell roamed the village streets day and night, wandering onto private property and invading gardens, it was only a matter of time before he'd stroll into homes as though he had a right to be there. She didn't want to walk into her cabin and find Caswell foraging in her food stores or sleeping in her bed.

Pink and orange tinged the sky. As the sun set, the eastern clouds faded to pale pink while those in the west brightened to a vibrant tangerine. Annie stood outside her door and watched the sky change colors until the sun dropped below the horizon. The sun's warmth evaporated with the fading light. Annie's breath created a visible puff of air when she sighed. She pulled her shawl around her shoulders and strolled toward the village while glancing every so often at the shadows.

By the time she reached the schoolhouse, the villagers were inside their homes, their fires burning and their candles lit. The village was most appealing at that time of day. Warm light shone from the windows, friendly and welcoming.

The schoolteacher, as always, had her one room at the rear of the schoolhouse brightly lit and her windows unshuttered. As far as Annie was concerned, the teacher issued a blatant invitation to those who would stand outside and stare in. Annie marched toward the cabin at the rear of the schoolhouse, mounted the two steps to the door, and rapped lightly.

Sarah, a thin pale woman with dark brooding eyes, flung open the door. Her long hair was tucked into a snood, anchored to the back of her head by ivory hairpins. Here and there, wavy strands hung loose about her face. Sarah stepped aside to let Annie enter, then shut and latched the door.

"You've left the shutters open again," Annie said. She dropped her shawl across a chair and removed her bonnet.

"Oh, I know; I'll close them." Sarah rushed to the window.

"Wait. I want to see out."

Sarah stepped aside and let Annie peer through the window. Reassured that no one lurked outside, she pulled the shutters closed and dropped the wooden bar into its notch.

Then she turned from the window and placed her bonnet on the chair with her shawl. "Sarah, why don't you make tea?" She walked past the teacher and examined a stack of papers that lay on the table. "You were marking the children's work?"

"Yes. I'm nearly finished." Sarah brushed by Annie and placed the cups and teapot on the table. She added loose tea to the pot and turned back to the fire to fetch hot water. Using a leather grip to grasp the metal handle, she lifted the kettle from the swinging fireplace hook and poured hot water over the tea leaves.

Annie sighed with pleasure. Having tea was a minimal requirement for all social interaction. She leafed through more of the papers as they quietly waited for the tea to steep. "The grades are quite high on these. Are you too easy on the children?"

"No. They're very bright." Sarah pulled out a chair and sat down at the table.

Annie smiled at her friend, thinking how lovely the young teacher was, how the older boys in Sarah's classroom must sigh when she looked their way. Wisps of Sarah's hair had escaped their restraints and lay against the creamy skin of her neck. Annie walked past the table and stood behind her. She reached out her hand and gently pulled Sarah's snood loose from her hair.

To Annie, Sarah seemed not one day older than the day they'd first met. Annie had been summoned to Philadelphia to settle the affairs of her only living relative, her father's youngest brother, and therefore agreed to remain an extra week to await the arrival of Miss Sarah Wallace, the new schoolteacher. Annie felt protective of her charge at first, like a mother hen. Only later did she realize she'd grown to love Sarah with all her heart in ways she could not describe, nor would she try.

Annie wasn't sure Sarah loved her in the same way, but she knew Sarah needed her. Nothing else mattered. After their tea and a leisurely meal taken by the fireplace, Annie and Sarah made sure the windows were shuttered and the bar placed across the door before they went to bed.

Early the next morning, in the darkest moments before the first gray light edged up from the horizon, Annie placed a log on the glowing embers in the fireplace. She gently shook Sarah's shoulder.

"I'm leaving now," Annie said. "Get up and set the latch after

I'm gone." She stopped before she opened the door and glanced back at Sarah. "It's Saturday."

"I know."

"The new bottle of whiskey you bought from the peddler? I poured it out while you were sleeping. It's empty." Annie closed the door softly behind her, before Sarah could respond.

CHAPTER TWENTY-THREE:
SARAH, ALONE AND LONELY

Sarah heard Annie drop a new log on the fire, felt the touch on her shoulder as Annie said she was leaving. Keeping her eyes closed, Sarah willed herself back to sleep so she could later wake up alone and pretend it had been that way all along.

But Annie insisted. "Get up and set the latch," she had ordered. Sarah rustled the covers and stuck one foot out to test the warmth of the room. Perhaps she could run to the door, latch it, and return to her bed before the bedding went cold.

But Annie spoke again. *Yes, of course it's Saturday,* thought Sarah. Annie didn't need to tell her so. As Sarah began to make sense of Annie's words, she burrowed under the covers and drew herself into a fetal position with her arms clasped across her belly. Sarah could not buy more whiskey for at least a week, not until the peddler returned. Yet Annie intended to walk out the door and leave Sarah alone with her fear, her melancholy, and her anger.

Sarah was not concerned about the whiskey itself. She had more hiding places in her room than Annie would ever find. What truly alarmed her, however, was the woman's continued interference in her life. After more than four years of Annie's occasional night visits, Sarah now understood how Annie controlled others, including Sarah, who she claimed to adore.

They'd first met when Annie arrived in Philadelphia to escort Sarah to her teaching job in the Village of Sangamon. Sarah had felt lost and alone, and appreciated the help when Annie stepped

forward and took charge. Now it seemed Annie would always
be in charge. When Annie saw the girls in the schoolyard bullied
by the boys, she chastised Sarah. When Sarah wept during the
preacher's prayer meetings, Annie admonished her. Annie
demanded their trysts be spontaneous and at Annie's conve-
nience, and always at Sarah's cabin.

Sarah was as isolated and alone as she'd ever been, whether
living with her father in India, or boarding at a girls' school
where no one liked her.

Why had she allowed herself to be seduced? She blushed and
put her hands on her cheeks to confirm the heat. Sarah
understood. Touch. The touch. At their first meeting Annie
clasped Sarah's hand and held it too long, warming Sarah's skin
so her palm became damp. Annie complimented Sarah's hair
and tucked a curl back behind her ear, sending tiny shivers
down Sarah's neck and shoulders. When they left Philadelphia,
Annie thrust her gloved hand through Sarah's crooked elbow
and guided her to their wagon, all the while allowing her hand
to rest gently against Sarah's side. As gentle fingers brushed her
breast, they triggered a tightening of Sarah's skin from her neck
to her thighs. Finally, alarmed by her reaction to Annie's friendly
behavior, Sarah pulled away on the pretext of checking her
bags.

Sarah liked her new friend. She assumed all of the women in
Sangamon would be as warm and friendly as Annie. If Sarah
feared touch, even as she craved touch, it was her own personal
problem. She would cope with change and adapt to her new
environment, as she'd dealt with past challenges.

Born in India in 1808 to a rigid British soldier and his frail
wife, Sarah had little contact with her mother, and only occasionally did she cross her father's path. Those meetings were
rarely pleasant.

"Stop it now," he shouted when Sarah had wept over a scratched knee. "Let her be," he barked at the nurse. "There'll be no fussing about. Don't want another flibbertigibbet in this house."

The nurse felt sorry for Sarah, especially when she caught the lonely child at an upstairs window, watching her mother doze on a chaise in the garden below, her attendant sitting close by. But Sarah's nurse was terrified by Major Wallace's open resentment toward India's climate, the Indian culture and people, and especially his own family. She stayed for Sarah's sake, but she obeyed the major when he ordered her not to mollycoddle the child.

By the time she was seven, Sarah had turned into a recluse. She ate alone, rarely went outside, and spent most of her time devouring books from her father's library. Thanks to a young, sympathetic British tutor, Sarah read the classics long before she could do simple arithmetic.

One day she lay on her bed, puzzling her way through her father's newly acquired copy of *The Travels of Dean Mahomet*, when the major strode into her room and stopped several feet short of her bed. He cleared his throat, began to speak, then noticed the book she'd chosen.

"How dare you," he snapped. He drew himself up, as stiff as though standing at attention before a superior officer. "Bring me that book."

Sarah scrambled off the bed and ran to her father. She held the book out to him. Her hand trembled. Tears stung the corners of her eyes, but Sarah willed them not to spill over.

"Never touch my books without permission. When you receive permission, make certain your hands are clean before taking the book from its shelf. Always return it to its proper position when you are finished."

Sarah had feared punishment of a worse sort, perhaps even

banishment from the library. "I will," she promised.

The major frowned. "Well, it hardly matters. I've come to tell you your mother is ill. You'll be returning to England with her by the week's end. I'll send a maid to help you pack your things."

He marched out of the room without another word.

The move proved to be a great disappointment to young Sarah. All that she'd read of England promised green meadows and rose-covered cottages in bucolic surroundings. Or grand mansions surrounded by wind-swept moors.

Sarah's reality, however, was a girls' boarding school in a converted manor in the heart of London. The mistress was strict, the dormitories freezing, and the food tiresome—not a hint of curry, or salt and pepper, for that matter.

Sarah's deficiency in math and science might have been ignored by other schools, but Pellie Holland's School for Girls was different. Mistress Holland's mission was to educate girls, especially those who were destitute or orphaned, to be teachers and assist them in finding employment.

The teachers were respectful of the students but not fond of them. There were no pats on the shoulder or hugs for a job well done. And the other students provided no comfort. Their answer to weepers and crybabies was always the same—they jumped on the offender and pounded on her until she learned how to gulp down her sobs and squeeze her eyes so the tears couldn't escape. Occasionally rumors raced through the school that a certain girl did nasty things, although Sarah had no idea what that pronouncement meant. She never developed close friendships, nor did she admire any of her teachers enough to develop a crush on one. Sarah remained innocent.

When Sarah's mother died two years later, Sarah found it made very little difference in her life. She heard nothing more from her father until she completed her education. He sent her five hundred pounds to help her get settled when she found a job. Sarah never heard from him again. Whenever she thought of him, she had to fight off a deep sadness that she had not succeeded in making him love her.

"Pennsylvania?" Sarah had exclaimed. "That's in America."

"Yes, that's where you're going," Mistress Holland had replied. "My brother is moving his family there one month from now. He has agreed to take you under his protection and accompany you as far as Philadelphia."

"I'll be alone in Philadelphia?" Sarah's voice rose and tears welled in her eyes.

Miss Holland sighed. "You're like a mouse, Sarah. My brother will deliver you to the doorstep of the Franklin Association of Teachers. You'll pay a small fee for room and board until they find you a school. The school will provide an escort to your new home."

Sarah pictured a large Philadelphia school where she could teach reading and writing to young children from well-to-do families, boys and girls with gentle manners and studious demeanors. She'd live alone, or with a gracious family, free of the loud, crude roommates with whom she'd boarded at Pellie Holland's school.

"It will be in the prairie lands, of course," said Mistress Holland. "New towns are springing up throughout the prairie states. Schoolteachers are in great demand. If you choose well, you'll be paid fifteen dollars a month and receive free room and board."

The ocean journey from England to New York, river and land travel to Philadelphia, a stay of several months while she secured a position, and finally on to the Village of Sangamon in the State of Illinois—Sarah was in a constant state of exhaustion, anxiety, and terror. If she wasn't dealing with bedbugs on the riverboats, she was throwing up from the change in food and water. The sight of an Indian sent her into a frenzy of shaking. After one keelboat caught fire and sank, Sarah was distraught the whole time she was on the river.

However, Annie Gray, the God-fearing woman sent to escort Sarah from Philadelphia to Illinois, stayed close by and intervened when any of the rough men they encountered approached.

By the time the two women arrived in Sangamon, they were friends. There remained nothing more between them until, nearly two years later, Sarah sat at her table on a Friday evening and drank sip after sip of the peddler's best whiskey. She thought of the children and how little she could teach them because of their erratic attendance. Boys whose cruelty extended to knife fights, sexual assaults on little girls, and threats against her life when she attempted punishment. Girls who had little to look forward to except marital servitude.

As always, Sarah began to cry.

Someone rapped sharply at her door.

It was dark and she'd left her shutters open again. She struggled to her feet and walked unsteadily across the room. Without a word, she opened the door, knowing she reeked of whiskey and might face an authority who could fire her on the spot.

But it was Annie. Annie who came into her room, gave her comfort, and stayed with her until morning. From then on, Sarah cried more than ever. But she never refused to let Annie in.

CHAPTER TWENTY-FOUR:
WHEN JOHN TRIES TO INTERVENE

John urged his pinto into a trot as he left Annie Gray's farm near Sangamon and headed south. He'd traveled at least ten miles before the flush left his face and his shoulders relaxed. He loosened his grip on the reins, slowed the horse to a walk, and stared into the distance. His first thoughts had been only of himself and the humiliation he'd suffered when Miss Gray cut off his proposal of marriage before he'd gathered the courage to speak. He turned the pinto back toward Sangamon and bumped the horse's sides with the heels of his boots.

"You must never insult a lady," his mother had taught him. "Next to your relationship with God, a respectful and honorable relationship with women will be the most important to sustain."

John was five years old the first time he had heard this message, shortly after he'd thrown a little girl's doll in the rain barrel.

He heard it again when he went to school, when his teacher reported John had a habit of yanking on the braids of the girl who sat in front of him.

Again and again, his mother reminded him of his obligations to those delicate creatures and warned him of the consequences of ungentlemanly conduct. Not that Annie Gray was in any way delicate. Even so, how could he ride away from Sangamon without apologizing and relieving the tension he'd injected into their friendship?

As John drew near the town, passing a few feet from the woods that bordered the bend in the river, the old Kickapoo Indian emerged from the trees and walked toward the road, seemingly oblivious to John's presence.

"Hello," John called out.

Fish stopped in his tracks, his eyes wide and mouth agape. When he saw John, he nodded a greeting, then stood beside the road and waited. John read the Indian's posture as giving up the right-of-way. With a jostle of the reins and a cluck of his tongue, John pushed his horse forward and stopped when he reached the old man.

"Greetings, Grandfather," he began in the Indian way. "Have you been well?"

"Good," Fish replied. "Long time since you came to this village."

"Yes, last August. Many things happened, and then I journeyed home to see my father."

"I heard the story. The Great Spirit came, made the lightning dance. That boy—"

"I want to ask you about that boy's sister," John said, anxious to avoid any further discussion of Caswell's injuries. "Annie Gray told me the girl is staying with you."

Fish straightened his shoulders, tilted his head back, and stared at John. "Annie Gray told you?"

"Yes."

"You did not tell others?"

"No, I won't tell others."

"Jo Mae is here. She can stay."

"Is she well?"

Fish shrugged. "Her body is not sick. She's very strong. But she does not talk. I think Jo Mae's spirit is sick."

"Perhaps I can help. May I speak with her?"

The Indian appeared to consider the question carefully before answering. Finally he raised his arm and pointed toward town. "If Annie Gray says you can talk to Jo Mae, then you talk, but you bring Annie Gray here."

John gently kicked the pinto's sides. He leaned forward in the saddle as his horse leaped ahead and galloped toward the village.

Annie Gray looked surprised when she opened the door to find him waiting, hat in hand. "I thought you'd left Sangamon," she exclaimed.

"I did indeed plan to be on my way."

"But you came back. Why?"

"The way I left . . . before . . . it disturbed me. I came back to make amends."

"Amends? For what?"

"I want to apologize. It was rude to jump up and rush out your door as I did. After I considered my behavior, I grew afraid our acquaintance would no longer be pleasant to you, that you might avoid my company. I don't want that to happen."

"Oh, John, I'm sorry you were upset. I'll not regard you any differently than I always did. You're our preacher, and you are well favored in our community, a friend to all. Set your mind at rest."

John let out the breath he'd held. Once again, she'd called him John, but he dared not respond in kind. "Thank you, Miss Gray. You are most generous."

"Not at all. Is there anything else? I have chores to do."

"One other thing. I spoke to Fish out on the road. He said I might go to his dwelling and talk to Jo Mae. He said you should come with me, to let him know you approve."

She frowned. "Is there a need for you to talk to the girl? The fewer people who are seen going from the town to Fish's home by the river, the less chance people will find out Jo Mae is there. I'm not sure Fish could protect her if her mother or Caswell finds out where she is.' "

"Fish told me she's not talking very much. This seemed to disturb him. He said she might be 'sick in spirit.' "

"I can't imagine Jo Mae feeling melancholy for long. She has more spirit than anyone I've ever known. However, I've not seen her yet and I promised Fish I would come soon. Could you stay in Sangamon tonight so we can slip quietly out of town at first light? It's too near evening now. Caswell will be creeping about."

"He wanders the town at night?"

"Occasional days, but most often nights. He avoids people, especially the children who make fun of him. But at the same time, he lurks in the shadows, peeks in windows."

"I'll speak to Mr. Pritchard about a bed."

"Don't wait for me in the morning. Saddle your horse and carry your bedroll and saddlebags. I'll make my way on foot from the back of my cow shed without going through town. We'll meet in the woods at the first bend in the river."

Once again John found himself alone in the tiny room behind the blacksmith shop. This time, however, he did not dwell on Caswell or the lightning strike that had knocked the boy to the ground. Nor was John's aborted marriage proposal to Annie Gray weighing on his thoughts, even though marriage had been advised by both his father and his minister as the path to a less self-absorbed existence.

His attention through the evening, ending only when he dropped into a dreamless sleep, focused on a young girl's starving soul. He, John Claymore, had the ability to feed that soul's hunger. When Jo Mae's baby was born, John had the power to save the baby from eternal darkness. His chest expanded with warmth as he foresaw the good he could do.

★ ★ ★ ★ ★

By the time John reached the bend in the river early the following morning, the sun pushed a hazy gray light above the horizon. As he rode up, Annie stepped out from the edge of the woods and motioned him to follow her into the trees. They stopped for a moment while John dismounted, and Annie peered toward the road to confirm no one had seen them.

John tied the pinto to a low-lying branch but remained by his horse as Annie signaled him to wait. They stood side by side, silent. The light grew, and suddenly Fish stood before them, as though he'd materialized from the mist.

Fish did not speak, but walked away, indicating they should follow. It took less than ten minutes to reach the hut. There Fish waved Annie Gray inside, but stood at the entrance with his arms crossed, barring John's way.

"Jo Mae is sleeping. You wait."

"Of course."

"You sit." Fish pointed to a large log that lay near a stone-lined pit a few feet away.

John sat down. "Do you have enough food? Blankets? For both you and Jo Mae?"

"Yes."

"And when the baby is born?"

"Annie Gray will come."

"Miss Gray said the baby will be born in February. It will be cold, maybe snow and ice. It might be difficult for Miss Gray to leave her farm. What if she cannot come? Will Jo Mae and the baby be warm? Well fed? Will the baby be safe?"

Fish raised his chin and frowned at John. "You think the baby is not safe here?"

"I don't know. Babies get sick and die even when they live in warm houses. Wouldn't Jo Mae and her child be more likely to survive if they lived in a house with white people?"

Fish snorted. "What white people? Jo Mae's mother does not love that girl. Jo Mae's brother has an evil spirit. The white people Annie Gray asked to take care of Jo Mae were not good people. Better for me to take care of Jo Mae and her baby."

"Grandfather, I was thinking of my own mother and father who live in New Salem. They are good people, very kind and most generous. Jo Mae and her baby would be well cared for."

"This New Salem is far away?"

"Two days' ride by horse and wagon."

"No. Too far."

Fish ended the conversation and turned to see what troubled the old dog. It had stumbled out of the hut and now stared into the woods, a low growl rumbling in its throat. Fish stood still, hardly appearing to breathe. John froze as well. The hairs rose on the back of John's neck as Fish glided into the trees with the dog limping close behind.

Annie Gray threw back the blanket covering the doorway of the hut and peered outside. John quickly put his finger to his lips before she could speak. She took a look around and then withdrew into the hut, dropping the blanket back over the opening. John stood facing the woods, unsure how he could protect the women inside but determined to try if necessary.

He heard nothing for several minutes, then was startled by something crashing through the brush. A few seconds later, Fish reappeared.

"What made that noise?" John asked.

"I don't know." Fish shrugged. "I did not see anything. Dog ran into woods but he is too slow."

"Could it have been Jo Mae's brother?"

Fish shrugged again but made no comment.

"May we come out now?" whispered Annie. "Or will you come inside?"

John waited until Fish gave him permission to enter.

"Go," said the Indian. "I will keep watch here."

Inside, the shelter appeared to have more space than its size suggested. With bedding folded away and utensils carefully stowed on wall hooks and shelves, the Indian had created the illusion of extra room where it did not exist. A fire crackled in the fire pit, warming the room far beyond John's expectations. Even so, he wondered whether that coziness could be sustained during a blizzard or subzero temperatures.

Annie and Jo Mae sat side by side on furs placed on the ground near the fire. As his eyes became accustomed to the dim interior light, John saw the child more clearly. Her appearance was much improved by her long-sleeved dress, leggings, and moccasins, all made of deerskin.

"You're looking at my clothes, aren't you? I sewed them. Fish showed me what to do and I did all he said, and he even fixed me a good needle out of a buffalo bone and made all this twine stuff by cutting the skins very thin. I did it all good, didn't I?"

"It's very good."

"Fish says I'm more like one of those other Indians, the Cherokee. They wear clothes lots different from Fish's people. He says the women of his tribe used to wear long skirts and shirts made out of cloth they'd weave all by themselves. He did not have the stuff to do that, but he said this would be lots better than wearing those same clothes I had every day because they were nearly worn thin as paper and it's getting cold out now."

John glanced at Annie and saw her staring at Jo Mae. Annie raised her eyebrows. "I thought Fish said she wasn't talking much," Annie said with a smile. "You seem to have brought the child out of her shell, John."

"Jo Mae," John said, "Fish told me he thought you might be sick in spirit."

"Me? I'm not sick."

"Well, maybe feeling bad about things that have happened to you."

"Like what? Being with child? Having a brother who's so evil he shouldn't be alive? That's not so bad. Look at that poor old dog out there with only three legs and one good eye, and Fish said Caswell did the hurting. Leastways he never did anything like that to me. But Preacher, when you threw the lightning at Caswell, I wanted to dance in circles and praise your name."

"Oh, but I didn't—"

"And having a mama who acts like she'd birthed an ugly old pig when she birthed me? Well, I guess anyone would feel bad about that.

"Preacher, I am not sick and I do not think God did these things to me because I'm bad, and I'm not going to quit trying to make things get better. Anyway, everything is already getting better since Fish let me live here. He and that old dog take care of me now, and as long as Mama and Caswell don't know I'm here, I'm thinking I'll be safe as can be, at least for a time."

John smiled. "Fish says you don't talk much, and that's why he thought you were sick."

"Well, Fish does not talk much, either. I thought maybe he'd get so tired of me going on and on that he'd make me go home to Mama, so I try to think more than I talk. That's not so easy. There's lots of questions I'd like to ask him, but I tell myself to only ask one time a day."

"I asked Fish about the winter and whether you and your baby will be safe and warm if the weather turns colder. It's only two days' ride to New Salem where my mother and father live. You would be warmly welcomed if you chose to go there."

"And leave Fish? After him being so good to me and teaching me how to sew and telling me about the Great Spirit and all? No, sir. I'm staying here."

"Even though Caswell is not far away?"

"Fish and old dog will watch over me. And besides, if Caswell comes to bother me again, I'm going to yell out loud for you to throw more of that lightning and this time you ought to strike that man dead because he's for sure one of Satan's devils if he's not Satan himself."

"Jo Mae," Annie said, "the preacher did not throw the lightning that hit the tree."

"Oh, Miz Annie, he sure did. I saw it myself, but his aim is not so good because he hit the tree instead of Caswell's head."

"No, I didn't throw the lightning, Jo Mae. It only appeared that way."

"You say what you want, Preacher, but I know what I saw."

John decided it best to change the subject. "Shall I come back to see you again when I return to Sangamon?"

"That would be good. When are you coming back?"

"Might be five or six months. Takes about that long to call on every town on my circuit."

"Well, if it takes that long, then this here baby will be born already." Jo Mae placed both hands on her abdomen and regarded her belly as though speaking directly to her unborn child. "What do you think of that, little baby? Next time Preacher comes to Sangamon, you can give him a big smile."

John felt the urge to reach out and put his hand on Jo Mae's swollen belly, to close his eyes and imagine the life growing within. He sucked in his breath, clasped his hands together, and bowed his head in a brief and silent plea for God to still the strange ideas that seemed to spring from his mind with no warning.

CHAPTER TWENTY-FIVE:
CASWELL LOSES CONTROL

Back and forth Caswell walked in the tiny cabin, his heavy boots clomping against the wooden planks, his fists squeezing hard. His mouth moved as he listed silent complaints against Mama and everyone else he blamed for his hunger.

Mama kept on sleeping.

He kicked the wall each time he crossed the room. He felt a crooked half-smile twist one side of his face when he heard the rustling of Mama's cornhusk mattress. When he saw her grow quiet, he thought she might fall back asleep, so he kicked one of the wooden legs of her bed.

"Stop it, Caswell."

Mama didn't even throw the covers back so she could see him. He kicked the bed again.

"Stop it!"

This time she pushed the blanket away from her face and glared at him as she clutched the blanket to her chest and tried to sit up. Even in the faint glow from the embers in the fireplace, Mama's face shone like a demon in the red light. Caswell sucked in his breath and held it as he stepped away from the bed.

"What's wrong?" Mama asked in that way Caswell hated, the way that said she thought he was bad and he would always be bad, and she wished he would go away and leave her alone.

He kicked the table leg. "I'm hungry."

Mama moaned and lay down, curling up on her side and tucking the blanket under her chin. "I'll go see Annie Gray

173

tomorrow, Caswell. I can't go now. It's the middle of the night."

"But I'm hungry now."

"Later, Caswell. Go back to bed."

Mama fell asleep before he could answer. Caswell stared at the pile of covers, thought of pulling her out of bed and making her go to Miz Gray's that very minute. Instead, he went to his own cot where he lay down without removing his boots. When the empty feeling in his stomach returned, and the gurgling noises grew louder, Caswell pushed himself up and sat on the edge of the bed. Finally he stood, took the worn gray blanket, and draped it over his head and shoulders.

He let himself out into the chill fall air, unable to see more than a few feet ahead because ground fog hid the town. A soft cloud closed in on him as it swirled and billowed in the dim light from the open cabin door. He tried to see into the fog but it was like trying to find his own thoughts.

He stayed outside but pulled the door closed. He saw things better when no light bounced off the fog. While he waited for his eyes to get used to the glare, he tried to think. It was hard. So many of the things he should know about kept getting away from him, like dust blowing around in his head. Bits and pieces would pop into his mind if he wasn't trying too hard, but most of the time he chased those bits and pieces here and there and never caught them. He closed his eyes and told his mind to wander on its own for a while.

Stealing eggs from Miz Gray's laying hens. Miz Gray had almost got him once. She'd come out of the schoolteacher's room while Caswell was still on his nighttime prowl. He followed her, staying well back so she wouldn't see him. She must have known he was there—she kept searching all around, trying to see into the shadows. Caswell snuck into the trees by the road and laughed loud enough for Miz Gray to hear. She took off running and didn't stop until she got to her own place. Next thing Caswell saw, Miz Gray stood in front of her door with a musket. He didn't make another sound until he got back home to Mama's cabin.

He couldn't stop thinking about stealing from the Injun's traps. Only the Injun had come close to catching him once. Caswell had thrown the stolen rabbit into the brush and run away as fast as he could. The Injun caught up with him, but by then Caswell was far away from the sprung trap. The Injun couldn't prove Caswell lied.

A catfish from one of the Injun's water traps? Mama wouldn't be so mean then.

He pulled the gray blanket tight under his chin with one hand and held the edges together over his chest with the other. He followed the road through the village until he reached the north edge of the woods, barely able to see ten feet in front of him. Standing still, hidden by the trees, he listened for signs the Injun was near. Caswell heard footsteps, then the whinny of a horse. He waited until the steps moved past. Not the Injun, he thought. Someone on the road. A moment later he thought he heard voices, but the sound was so faint, he wasn't sure. Then the quiet returned.

As he moved deeper into the trees, he found it easier to make his way. The fog had lifted to waist high in places, so there was less chance he would trip and fall. Even so, he crept along, one step at a time, holding onto branches or leaning against tree trunks to steady his balance.

His gray blanket was the same color as the thick mist. He moved closer to the Injun's camp, able to see little more than his own feet and the nearest trees and bushes. Caswell figured out he should look for the traps closest to the Injun's camp while it was still hard to see and while the Injun was likely asleep.

As he drew near the clearing by the river, he once again heard voices. He stopped. Then, as quiet as he had ever been in his life, he tiptoed closer and peered through the brush. The fog was thicker by the river, but the campfire lit the small clearing so it looked pink and fuzzy like a place where ghosts would live.

The Injun stood in front of his hut with his arms crossed. Another man sat on a log by the fire, but Caswell could only see his back. Caswell leaned down and picked up a dried branch from a dead tree. Not sure why he did it, he hurled the piece of wood through the air toward the opposite side of the clearing.

The limb barely missed the camp, bouncing off a tree. It attracted the Injun's attention and lured the dog outside. They entered the woods on the other side of the hut. Annie Gray poked her head out of the doorway and spoke to the other man. The man stood and walked over to the hut, turned, and faced the clearing.

Caswell gasped when he recognized the preacher. He shrunk back as he pulled the blanket over his head and lifted it high enough to see the ground in front of him. The Injun and the dog were forgotten. Getting away from the preacher became the only thing on Caswell's mind. He took off through the woods and did not stop until he reached the road that led back to the village. There he paused to catch his breath and drop the blanket to his shoulders.

The sun was now visible as a pale yellow circle glowing through the mist. It seemed to sit on top of Miz Gray's cabin at the far end of Sangamon. The fog had moved higher, now floating above his head. Caswell stepped onto the road and hurried home. He burst into the cabin, threw himself onto his cot, and pulled his blanket over his head. He did not sleep, but huddled there, trembling, until Mama finally woke up.

As she dumped logs into the fireplace and poked life into the fire, she used the poker to smack at the end of Caswell's cot. "Get up, Caswell."

He pulled the blanket away from his face and scooted down to the end of the cot to warm himself at the fire.

Mama stood with her hands on her hips, the poker swinging gently back and forth against her leg. She banged the poker against the floor to get his attention. "What's the matter with you? You sick?"

"Nothing's the matter, Mama." But still he sat, his mind on his trip to the woods, the people gathered at the Injun's camp, the preacher who'd nearly killed him with his arm of fire. He couldn't figure out what those three were doing there together. It made his head hurt to think about it. He frowned at Mama. He was mad at her, wasn't he? He squinted his eyes and stared hard. What had made him want to drag Mama out of bed?

"I'm hungry, Mama. You're going to see Miz Gray . . . but . . . oh, Mama, you. . . ."

He couldn't think what to say. He didn't want to tell Mama he'd been roaming around in the woods, trying to steal from the Injun's traps.

It was nearly daylight outside, so he couldn't go steal from Miz Gray's farm. She'd be after him with her musket for sure. Confusion grabbed at his head, ripping out his good thoughts and throwing them here and there faster than he could grab them back.

His ideas were all mixed up again. He tried to sort things out. His stomach growled. It made him mad that Mama stood there with her mouth pinched up and didn't say anything while she kept thumping the poker against the floor. It shamed him to feel tears stinging his eyes. It was too much.

He grabbed the fireplace poker out of Mama's hand and threw it across the room. With two hands, he upended the table and pushed it over. Then he faced Mama, his hands working to clench and relax, clench and relax. When Mama turned and ran for the door, he reached out and grabbed her nightgown at the hem. Jerked up short, Mama lost her balance and fell, banging her head against the table before she hit the floor.

Mama didn't move. Caswell tried to figure out what he should do next. He walked across the room and picked up the poker.

For a few minutes he stood, worrying she wouldn't ever get up. He thought she might be sleeping. As his breathing slowed, the mixed-up words got together in his head. He raised the poker and stared at it. He looked at his mother, crumpled on the floor. Then he leaned the poker against the stones by the fire. He went back to Mama's side, bent down, and stroked her hair.

"Mama, Mama, wake up."

He patted her cheek.

"You'll feel better in a minute, Mama."

Caswell lifted her in his arms, and carried her to her bed. As he pulled up her covers, he saw her eyelids move, and then her eyes open. He stepped back and clapped his hands together.

"You're awake. Mama, go to Miz Gray's house now. I'm hungry."

She frowned and put her hand to her head, then glanced toward the fireplace where the poker leaned against the wall. She sat up and swung her legs from the bed to the floor.

"Go on outside now. I'm getting dressed."

"You're going to Miz Gray's for food?"

"Yes."

"Okay. I'm going outside now."

Minutes later, even before Mama put on her clothes and came out the door, Caswell saw the preacher in the distance, riding into the village as though he'd come from the south road instead of the river. When Caswell looked the other direction, he saw Miz Gray walking from her back shed toward her cabin.

He puzzled on that for a few minutes. The Injun's traps. The

Injun and the old dog must be back there at the camp all alone. Mama didn't get much meat from Miz Gray. Caswell wanted meat.

He wanted to go back to the woods, but he would pass the preacher if he went straight through the village. As he stood there, wondering where to go, the preacher got off his horse, tied the reins around the hitching post, and walked into the general store.

Caswell made his way to the blacksmith shop, snuck around the back, and continued out of town until there were no more buildings to hide behind. From there, he moved as fast as he could, checking behind him every few seconds.

Once in the woods, he followed the same path he'd taken earlier until he reached the edge of the Injun's camp. He leaned against a tree and waited. He was still there, waiting and watching, when the Injun walked out of his shack and picked up a sprung trap that lay on the ground by the doorway.

Then Jo Mae and the dog came outside. She waved goodbye to the Injun as he walked away.

CHAPTER TWENTY-SIX:
JO MAE AND THE GREAT SPIRIT

The Indian who was my friend told me he was called Fish because catching fish was how he lived. I guessed that went for me too, so if I had an Indian name, maybe it should be Little Fish. Big Fish gave me blankets and a corner of his one big room where I slept close to the dog to keep warm. Fish gave me food and water every day, and he told me stories like he had always done about the Kickapoo and how the homes belong to the women because they built them themselves, and how women went off to a special *wikiyapi* for birthing babies and the men stayed away.

And he told me how it came to be that when the soldiers told the Kickapoo they had to leave the prairie and move to the other side of this really big river by St. Louis, and then they had to walk a long, long way, well, Fish would not go. He hid in the woods so the soldiers would not find him, and then he kept moving on for a long time, looking for the right place to stay. He built this little house, and he stayed right here on the Sangamon River.

Fish never once bothered me in a bad way and never asked me one question about why I hid from folks. He never told anyone in town that I lived here except Miz Gray, and I reckon she's the one who told Fish about me being with child because he already knew about that before I even told him. I guess Miz Gray told the preacher about everything too, because they both came to see me at the same time.

"Please, please, promise not to tell where I am," I told the preacher. "My mama would probably want to take my baby away, and Caswell would surely beat me or kill me or even make me go back and do things that are so bad—"

"Shhh, Jo Mae," he said, talking so soft I did not hardly hear him. I could not tell if he wanted to make my fears go away, or if he did not want to hear one more word about the terrible things I'd been doing, which I was also going to tell him were Caswell's fault. I surely would not have thought of awful things like that on my own.

"I'll not tell a soul," he said.

"And I'll come to check on you whenever I can," Miz Gray said.

I felt better then. "Don't let Caswell see you," I said to Miz Gray. "With him doing all that wandering in the night and peeking at people, he'll follow you for sure."

She acted like she knew exactly what I was talking about, so then I knew she would be careful, and she would keep her word. She is truly a good, kind woman.

The day the preacher and Miz Gray came to see me was not a good day, but it did not have anything to do with them. It happened when they were gone, after I was talking to Fish while he got ready to check on his traps.

I followed him out the door and watched him take off walking along the river, and I was hoping he'd bring back fresh meat for a big stew we could make with the potatoes and carrots Miz Gray brought us. I jumped near a foot when I heard a noise in the bushes. I looked that way as quick as can be, because I was ready to run like the wind if a big animal came, but I did not see anything at first.

All of a sudden two branches were being pulled apart, and I saw the ugly, mean face of my horrible brother, Caswell, scaring me near to death. I ran inside where Fish keeps an old skinning

knife, and while I was running as good as I could, I heard crashing and cracking sounds in the woods and figured Caswell ran
just as hard the other way. I slowed down and took a deep
breath, but that did not help chase away the feeling I had on my
skin, like it was covered with little crawly bugs. Goes to show
how everything going on in a person's life can change fast as
the teeth on one of Fish's traps can snap shut. I was not sure
what would happen next, and I was scared for a long time after
that day.

Miz Gray did what she said. She brought food and clothes and
blankets and made sure I knew to boil water for a long time, so
I would not get sick and hurt the baby growing inside me. She
told me I'd best remember to keep on boiling the water long
after the baby was born, because even if I gave my baby my
own milk, I could make the baby sick by drinking bad water. I
know my eyes got big, and I did not know whether to believe
that. It was something I would have to think on. I guessed I'd
do what she said, since she knew a lot about birthing babies
even if she'd never been a mama herself.

I told her about Caswell seeing me from the woods, but Miz
Gray said that Mama had not mentioned a thing and that we
should stay watchful. I think she figured Caswell had already
forgotten he saw me, but she said if he came back and bothered
me, I could go stay at Miz Gray's house because she had a
couple of guns and would protect me.

But I wanted to stay with Fish. He felt like family to me. I
was not so sure that Miz Gray would make me feel like that. As
soon as my child was born and got old enough, I would have to
leave. We could not hide down there by the river forever. Sooner
or later, Mama or Caswell would be out to get me. I reckon
they'd both been missing whatever money Caswell got from
those men behind the stables. Even if Caswell was too stupid to

trade with men who wanted to poke at me back there in Sanga-mon, he could still beat on me whenever he could catch me.

I thought about the preacher some more, too, and what he said about going to stay with his daddy and mama and that they would take good care of me even before my baby came. I had told him I wanted to stay with Fish, but if my baby would be safer away from Sangamon, then I figured by the time the preacher came back on his big old spotty horse, I'd be ready to leave.

I'd be wanting Fish to go with me if I went, so I did not know what I was going to do. I just did not know.

I thought maybe Fish wanted to move on somewhere around that Missouri he always talked about. I could go along and learn how to build a *wikiyapi* and how to talk Kickapoo and maybe Fish would let me and my baby be his family since his own family all died. I could take care of him when he got old, like he's taking care of me in my time of trouble.

Since I'd been staying with Fish, I'd been getting mixed up about who was God and who was the Great Spirit and if the Kickapoo prophet was a real person or not, because Fish kept on talking about following him somewhere. I did not know if that prophet lived in Missouri, or on the other side of Missouri, or if he was someplace else like God, wherever that is.

Even with being mixed up about who I prayed to, I learned to think good thoughts and maybe even to love God in my heart like the preacher said. Or the Great Spirit like Fish said. One thing did not matter to me, and I always hoped it did not matter too much to God, and I did not think it mattered to the Great Spirit either, and that thing was how much I wished I would never see Caswell again.

I knew it would be better no matter where I'd go, whether it be with the preacher or with Fish, because if I was not anywhere near that ugly, evil Caswell, I would be a better person. It was a sure enough thing that if he came around there again, I would start wishing him dead and maybe thinking of ways to make that happen.

And that was, for sure, not a kind or loving way.

Chapter Twenty-Seven:
Mary's Father Comes to Sangamon

Mary heard Caswell calling long before his awkward steps sounded on the wooden stoop in front of her cabin. She glanced helplessly at the tall, white-haired man, her father, who now warmed his hands before her fireplace. She rested her hands in her lap and waited, resigned to the meeting about to take place.

"Mama, Mama," Caswell shouted as he lunged through the door, "I saw Jo Mae."

Mary saw him stop short when he saw a stranger in the room. Glancing from her father to Mary and then back again, Caswell seemed to forget the urgency of the news he'd brought. He sidled closer to Mary's side and said, "Mama, who is that?"

She said, "Your grandfather. His name is James Archer."

Her father stepped away from the warmth of the fire and stared at Caswell. Father raised his eyebrows but his expression remained impassive. Even so, Mary knew what he thought, knew the judgment he'd pass on her son would be one more mark against her.

"What's wrong with him?"

"An accident. Lightning struck a tree. Caswell was standing nearby."

"The preacher done it!" shouted Caswell. "You know he did, Mama."

Her father raised his eyebrows a little higher, but said nothing. Caswell gaped at the older man again. "Who is that, Mama?" he repeated.

"This is my father, your grandfather."

"Oh." Caswell transferred his attention to the round loaf of bread that sat uncovered on the table.

"Go outside now," Mary told him. She tore a chunk off the loaf and handed it to him. "Go on. I want to talk to my father."

Caswell threw one more glance toward her father, still standing at the fireplace. Then he ripped off a piece of bread with his teeth and shoved it into his mouth, smacking his lips loudly as he ran outside and slammed the heavy door behind him.

Her father saw the small clumps of black muck Caswell had tracked from the door to the table, but again he made no comment. Instead, he turned his gaze on Mary, where she still sat with her hands in her lap.

"What did he mean? Who's Jo Mae?"

Mary waved her hand dismissively and changed the subject. "I can't believe you're here. It's been almost twenty years. I'd given you up as dead a long time ago."

"Mary, I tried to find you. I didn't know where you were. You knew I'd been arrested. Adam did come to see you?"

"Yes."

"And he told you your mother died?"

"He did. After that I heard nothing more. I feared for your life and I didn't know what to do."

"There was nothing you could have done, Mary. I thought they were going to hang me without a trial. Then one day, a few months after the war ended, without explanation, they set me free. I immediately gathered the few possessions I had left and went to Ohio, hoping to set a great distance between myself and those former friends of mine who had failed to speak up in my defense. I took whatever work I could find and saved what I could, traveling farther west with each new opportunity. I lingered too long, it seems. By the time I reached Fort Dearborn, you were gone. No one remembered you."

"It was not safe in the north," she replied. "The Indian threat was too great."

"I also felt I would avoid the Indian wars if I traveled south. By then, I'd saved enough to establish myself in a trade. I hauled milled lumber, tools, nails, whatever a man needed to build a house, to wherever folks had grown tired of their log cabins and craved a more civilized abode.

"Everywhere I went, Mary, I asked about you and your son. I tracked you to LaSalle, but lost the trail. I found out no more until I chanced on a group of men who want to organize a huge migration into the West. They plan to move thousands of families by wagon train. I met a French trapper by the name of Montagne . . ."

"Ooh." The soft cry escaped Mary's mouth before she could suppress the sound.

"You remember him?"

"What did he say?"

"Just that he'd come across you and the boy and he'd brought you here where he thought you'd be safe."

"Nothing more?"

"No. What more would he say?"

"I don't know. It doesn't matter. Father, I don't mean to seem inhospitable. I'm in shock. Here you are, and I can't think what to say."

Her father observed her as though conducting an inspection. Her gown was worn and patched, her hemline grimy, her bodice food-stained, and her hair unkempt.

Mary bit her lip as she looked around the room, seeing her life through his eyes—the makeshift furniture with wobbly legs, the dirty floor, and the empty shelves.

"You baked that?" James asked, pointing at the loaf of bread.

Mary laughed, but with self-derision. "No, Father. I have no flour, no lard, no salt. Caswell is not able to work. I depend on the charity of my neighbors."

"Mary, do you not work at a trade? I sent you enough money to get started. What did you do with it?"

"I spent all the money you sent years ago. It would have been used up sooner if not for the kindness and generosity of those who have helped me when times were hard."

Her father stared at her face for so long without saying anything, she finally blushed and turned away.

However, instead of the harsh pronouncement she expected, her father only sighed and muttered, "You live like a pauper. Why didn't you use your money to buy a piece of land and grow your own food, or set yourself up with a spindle and loom? You could have purchased cotton and wool—"

"I suffer from headaches that put me in bed for days. I don't see well enough to read or sew or weave. I'm not strong enough to dig up the ground or work long hours in the sun. I hoped Caswell—"

"But you don't think that now," he exclaimed. "How long has he been like this?"

"Three, maybe four months. At first I thought he would get better . . . then when I realized nothing would change, I didn't know what to do."

"Thank God you have no other children."

Mary ignored the comment and changed the subject. "What's to happen now, Father?"

"I want to talk to the men of this town and the farmers around here, too, see if there's enough demand to warrant building a sawmill. If not here, then perhaps closer to St. Louis. I'll take my wagons back to Ohio and pick up more supplies. I expect to return by April or May at the latest."

"And the wagon trains to the West?"

"Idle talk, I think. Perhaps in a few years." He hesitated and then said, "Mary, do you want to come with me?"

"And Caswell?"

He shook his head.

"Then, no. I can't bear to be with him, but neither could I bear to leave him here alone. I often think it would have been better if . . ." She could not continue.

"I find it difficult to walk away when you're living like this." Her father waved his hand at her cabin, but the gesture seemed to take in her whole world of misfortune. "But I won't take care of you and that boy unless you change your ways."

He picked up his coat and hat from the chair by the fireplace, leaned toward Mary for a moment as though he might speak, and finally kissed her on the cheek. "I'll sleep by my wagon, outside the town. When my business is finished, I'll move on. I hope to see you much improved when I return."

With that, he stomped out the door and pulled it closed behind him.

Mary walked to the fireplace and used the poker to idly jab at the charred logs. When the fire flared, she added a fresh chunk of wood, then sat down in her rocking chair to stare into the flames. It had been years since anything had occurred in Mary's life that surprised her, but when she'd opened her door to that firm knock and found her father standing there, she'd been stunned.

Mary thought back to her father's rebuke and the warning that accompanied it. *He wants me to change my ways,* she thought. *He wants me to work.* She rubbed her palms together, stroking the chapped skin on the backs of her hands. She thought of Annie Gray's tanned and leathery skin and the calluses on her fingers. Mary touched her hair, fingering the ratty tangles she'd not brushed in weeks. Why did she fret so about her hands when she no longer cared for herself in any of the ways that had once mattered so much?

The girl who had gaily attended balls in colorful gowns of

silk and lace, the girl she'd once been, had turned into this. Mary smoothed the wrinkles in her skirt and picked at the frayed edge of her sleeve.

A noise outside the door distracted her from her reverie. Caswell. What had he tried to tell her when he first came in, before he'd been distracted by the strange man in his house? Something about Jo Mae.

Life hadn't been so hard before Jo Mae left. Mary considered how her situation might improve if Jo Mae returned, if she could be persuaded she had an obligation to her mother and brother. Jo Mae could work for Annie Gray in exchange for food and other needs for the family. Then Mary would not be "living like this," as her father had put it.

What had Caswell said when he came in the door? She remembered. Caswell had shouted out, "I saw Jo Mae."

Mary jumped up and hurried to the door, pulled it open, and went outside. Caswell sat on a large rock beside the road. He stood up as Mary came out the door, and stepped from one foot to the other.

"Is that man coming back, Mama?"

"He's gone for now. Caswell, when you came home before, you said you saw Jo Mae?"

"Yeah, Mama, I saw Jo Mae."

Mary waited, but Caswell didn't volunteer anything else. Finally she asked, "Where, Caswell? Where did you see her?"

"Down by the river. With the Injun."

"What was she doing there?"

"I don't know, Mama. She just stood there."

"Anyone else with them?" Mary heard the edge in her tone— the edge that often crept into her voice when she tried to carry on a conversation with Caswell.

"Early this morning there was."

"Who?" Mary shouted. "Who was there?"

"Well, I saw that preacher that hit me with the lightning."

As Mary's frustration grew, she had a sense of Caswell's speech slowing down, almost a feeling his brain slowed.

"Who else was there, you dolt?" she screeched. "Tell me!"

Caswell's jaw went slack and copious amounts of saliva drooled from his mouth as he gawked at his mother. He stammered, "Jo Mae . . . the Injun . . . the preacher . . . Miz Gray. That's all, Mama."

"Where were they?"

"Down by the river. I said that."

"Yes, but where? Near to town?"

"No."

"Caswell, I swear I'm going to smack you on the head if you don't tell me exactly where you saw Jo Mae."

He ducked his head as though assuming she would follow through on her threat before he'd had time to answer her question. With both arms protecting his ears, his head bent low to protect his face, he mumbled a string of words Mary didn't understand.

She tilted her head back and gritted her teeth, trying to calm her aggravation so she could pry this last bit of information from him. "Can you tell me exactly where you saw Jo Mae and the rest of those people?" she asked. "If you took me there, where would we go?"

Caswell raised his head to sneak a quick look at her from beneath his arms. Apparently satisfied that he was no longer in danger of getting hit, he said, "They were at the Injun's camp."

Mary's first inclination was to rush out to the Indian's hut immediately, and if she found Jo Mae, to drag her home whether the girl wanted to come or not. After a moment's thought, she reconsidered. It would take planning. She needed a persuasive argument to use on Jo Mae. She must offer her daughter something of value, a gift she could not turn down.

Mary turned her back on Caswell and walked into the cabin. A small tarnished brass pot sat on the mantel. She pulled it down and tipped the lid back on its hinge. Dipping her fingers inside the pot, she pulled out a tiny deerskin pouch. A gentle squeeze confirmed the gold nugget given to her by Henri remained inside. She shoved the pouch back into the pot and replaced it on the mantel as Caswell plaintively called, "Want to go see Jo Mae?"

Mary ignored him, shut the door, sat in her rocking chair, and thought about what she should do.

CHAPTER TWENTY-EIGHT:
JO MAE NAMES HER BABY

There were two deep snows during the winter when 1833 was done and 1834 began, but I hardly knew when one year turned into the next. Fish and me and the old dog were huddled by the fire pit most of the time. We watched the smoke twirl up and draw Kickapoo pictures of horses and Indian braves and good spirits before it disappeared through the fire hole and got blown away into the freezing cold air outside.

I listened to Fish's stories about when he was a boy and the special things that happened when he became a man, and more stories about his son who would not do what the old men in the tribe wanted, and so he got killed by soldiers. All that happened a long time ago, before this territory became the State of Illinois, which I did not know about and still do not much understand. I figured it's a funny thing to learn about territories and states and soldiers killing Indians from Fish instead of going to school and learning it from the schoolteacher.

I wanted to go out in the snow to help Fish with the traps. When I helped him before, I'd tote the things he caught in a bag, which sometimes got so full I had to drag it along the ground instead of carrying it. But when the second snow came before the first had melted some, I could not do it any longer.

Fish had used a flat pan to clear the snow away from the doorway and make a little circle around the outside fire pit, and that made the snow pile deep as my middle. Past that first pile of snow, which I had to climb over, it was still up almost to the tops of my knees. If I stepped out into it, I'd sink like a big rock. With my stomach sticking out in front, I could not get one foot up high enough to take another step, so I was stuck there until Fish pulled me out. Then he had to dig around in the snow to find the deerskin boots he gave me. My feet pulled right out of them because they were big enough boots for a grown woman. I reckoned they might have belonged to Fish's wife who died a long time ago, but I never did ask him about that, because I learned it's not polite to ask questions.

It did not matter that I was not helping Fish check the traps, I reckon, because he could not catch much in those traps anyway, being that the traps fell down through the snow. Fish said most of the furry creatures were hiding away in their holes in the ground. The river froze hard too, so Fish had to cut a hole in the middle where the water was deeper, and there he could sometimes catch a catfish, which tasted mighty good to me, even if it was one of the big ones that tasted like mud more than it tasted like fish.

We did not have to worry much about starving to death. Fish had worked extra hard before winter to cut lots of meat into strips and then dry them by the fire. Miz Gray brought us dried apples and some turnips and carrots. They'd last a long time where Fish buried them in the cold ground next to the woods.

Throwing bits of meat and vegetables in a pot with water and cooking it a long time made a satisfying meal, but one thing we learned real quick, and that was not to put in a handful of Miz Gray's dried apples. They had worms in them. Those worms came to the top and floated there, all white and squishy look-ing, and it was not too satisfying to see that. After that hap-pened one time, we changed to picking the apples apart and throwing the worms away and just eating the apple pieces. It was filling once you swallowed, but chewing those pieces was like chewing on a rag and surely did not taste much better. We did not tell that to Miz Gray, though.

It seemed like a long time that Miz Gray could not get out to see me, but I did not keep track of the days and nights so I was not sure. I did know that it was getting harder and harder to move around, and the clothes I wore were so tight I was afraid I would bust right out. I felt more like sleeping than talking, and when I was awake, I wanted to eat a lot more than I wanted to talk. Even if it's hard to believe, most of the talking during the snow time was being talked by Fish.

The story I liked the best was the one he told about the Great Spirit getting mad at all the Indian tribes for letting the White Man chase the Indians off their own land.

He said the Great Spirit gave land to the Indian tribe—all the water, all the prairie, all the buffalo and deer. Fish said the Great Spirit told the Indians to watch over the land. Then the White Man came. They killed Indians, stole land, and killed the buffalo. They even left the buffalos on the prairie for the vultures.

Fish would make wrinkles in his forehead like he could not understand the White Man's crazy-acting ways, wasting all that good buffalo meat, and the bones they could have used for tools and needles and such, and the buffalo skins like the one Fish had, which was the warmest kind of blanket a person could want.

"Great Spirit angry," Fish said, almost sounding like he was singing the story instead of telling it. "Shake earth, one day, two days, more. Indian tribe much afraid. *Wikiyapi* fell down, the horses broke loose from their ropes. The great river the White Man calls Mississippi ran the wrong way. The Great Spirit saw the White Man's house fall down, saw the fire burn across the prairie. But nothing changed in the White Man's heart. More came. They rode horses. Came in wagons and boats. Nothing could stop the White Man. Nothing.

"The Great Spirit blessed the tribe and made it keeper of the right way. He said when the White Man finds the end of the earth, all will die. The Indians, who know the right way, will still live. Indian tribe will come back, live on the prairie. Buffalo and deer will come back."

When Fish told this story, I always pretended I was a Kicka-poo Indian, and that when the end of the White Man came, I would still be alive. I would get to see the buffalo, which I told Fish I have never seen and could not picture in my head, even when he told me what they looked like.

A day came when the sun beat down and the air got all warm, like maybe the winter was going away. It was only the last week of January, which I would not have known. Miz Gray told me when she rode her mule out to the woods after the snow on the road melted a bit, and horses and wagons could get by. Even if Miz Gray did have to wade through some snow and a little mud, she did it, and she dragged along a sack of food, which did have more of those dried apples in it, but I did not say anything.

She also brought two more blankets she'd quilted all by herself from scraps of old clothes and feed sacks and such. They had so many colors and such fine sewing that I never did let that old dog sleep on top of them, but I did pull the covers over his back when it was freezing cold.

I was glad to see Miz Gray. My head was full of questions about what would happen if the baby started to come and Fish could not get to Sangamon to fetch her, and what should I do, and what should Fish do. Fish watched me like he thought my brain had bust loose, and I threw words out so fast he could not understand a thing those words were saying. Anyway, it was more words than I'd probably spoken since the second big snow came, so I could understand why he looked at me so funny.

Then Miz Gray got me to quit talking so much, and she told

me all the answers to my questions. Next, she sat down with Fish and told him all the same things she told me and more, but she made sure he understood everything she said. I could see he was a mite upset that he might have to help birth this baby if the weather turned to winter again, but he never said a word, just clamped his lips together and folded his arms across his chest and listened to Miz Gray's every word, while she talked as slow as she would if she was talking to a little child. I thought he knew what he had to do, even if an old Kickapoo man surely never had to help birth babies before.

While I listened to all these things that Miz Gray said, I got to thinking about Mama. I wondered if it was Caswell's daddy who helped Mama when Caswell was birthed, and then I got to thinking about when I was being born and wondered who helped Mama then. I did not have a daddy that I knew of, and so then I said out loud what I was wondering, just when Miz Gray thought she was all done talking and was getting ready to leave.

"I don't know about your mother when Caswell was born," she said. "That was long before she came to Sangamon. But when you came into this world, I was there. And you weren't but a few hours old when Fish showed up, so he got to see you on your very first day."

"Did I have a daddy?"

"I don't know, child. Your mother never told me who your father might be."

"Was Caswell there?"

"He sure was. You hollered so much when you were born that you nearly scared Caswell to death."

And that's all she or Fish would ever say about the day I was born, but she looked kind of funny when I asked about my daddy. I figure she might know more than she said, so I reckoned I'd ask her again someday.

Not much more than a week later, I got to having these big grabbing pains at my belly, and then I wet myself all over one of Miz Gray's quilts. I rolled over on my side and yelled to Fish that he'd better do something quick because I thought I was going to die without ever growing up or seeing my baby. I think maybe Miz Gray forgot to tell me how bad birthing-a-baby pains could be, but I do not see how it would have mattered, because a person cannot change her mind about a thing like that.

It was easy to see that Fish was of two minds about this whole business because first he said he'd go get Miz Gray, and he went outside, but when I yelled real loud with one of those pains, he turned around and came right back. He brewed me a horrible smelling medicine that I was supposed to drink like tea. He said Miz Gray told him it would help, but I never found out if it would or not, because I couldn't swallow it no matter how hard I tried and, believe me, I tried hard.

Fish went to leave again, and I yelled again, and finally Fish shrugged his shoulders and came back inside and started getting all kinds of things ready, just like Miz Gray had told him to. And it turned out that my friend, an old Indian man named Fish, was the first person to see my little baby girl, and he cleaned up my baby and gave her over to me, her new mama.

When I put that tiny little baby to my breast, Fish smiled and got a little tear in his eye. But then he turned as red as the head on a cock pheasant and went outside the cabin, leaving me all alone with the little baby I decided to name Annie after Miz Annie Gray, who had been good to me.

Fish then stuck his head back in the door and told me he'd go and get Annie Gray, but he'd leave the old dog in the cabin with me so I'd have some protection in case of trouble. I did not know what kind of protection I'd get from that poor old dog. He was getting so old he could not hardly run.

★ ★ ★ ★ ★

After that, Fish talked about moving on, but he said we'd stay put until it was for sure spring and there would not be any more snow. He'd try to wait for the preacher to come back, too, because maybe the preacher could help us decide where to go. So we stayed.

While we were waiting for spring to happen, with flowers and everything, it was the sweetest, most peaceful time I'd ever had in my whole life. I did not have anything to do but take care of little Annie and watch how she changed a bit almost every day. I was holding her in my arms and looking into her eyes the very day she curled her little mouth up and smiled at me for the first time. That one little tiny thing made me get warm all over and tears drip from my eyes, and I smiled back and stuck my nose on the soft skin of her neck and kissed little Annie and told her I loved her and would take care of her forever and ever.

CHAPTER TWENTY-NINE:
MARY WELCOMES SPRING

One day of thinking rolled into another day of plotting, but before Mary could settle on a plan to bring Jo Mae home, the weather intervened. When the first snow came, none of the villagers realized this winter would be another like the winter of 1830, which had been one of the hardest to hit central Illinois in years. Blizzard winds accompanied days of heavy, wet snow. By the time the winds died down and the sun came out, drifts as tall as two men buried the south and west sides of all of the buildings in the village.

One small shed on Annie Gray's farm toppled over from the weight of the snow, killing seven of the laying hens inside. The rest froze to death. Two of the frozen chickens, plucked and gutted by Annie, made it into Mary's cooking pot as soon as Annie could use her mule and harrowing board to flatten a walking path into Sangamon.

If not for Annie Gray's largesse, as well as the generosity of two other farmers who lived near Sangamon, the whole town might have died of cold and starvation, as no wagonloads of food or staples were able to reach Sangamon for three full months.

By then, Mary was far more concerned with maintaining a fire in her fireplace and keeping herself and her son fed than she was with finding Jo Mae and bringing her home.

However, there came a spring day early in April of 1834, when the snow melted on the roads and the sun shone warm on

Mary's face. As she'd searched on her mantel for her hairbrush, which she had mislaid, her eyes lit on the brass pot and its contents. That reminded her of Jo Mae, who should be living in her mother's house and not with that filthy heathen. Mary called Caswell inside and told him she wanted to go to the Indian's camp.

Caswell hadn't mentioned Jo Mae in months, so he reacted to her pronouncement with a blank stare. After a moment or two, his expression gradually changed. Mary could almost see comprehension lighten his features, like sunlight upon the passing of a cloud's shadow.

"Okay, Mama."

Mary put on her bonnet and draped her heaviest shawl across her shoulders. When she reached the doorway, she regarded the muddy road outside, kicked off the shoes she wore, and pulled on an old pair of Caswell's boots. Then she followed Caswell down the road, through the village and into the woods.

CHAPTER THIRTY:
JO MAE'S LIFE CHANGES

I could not hardly put that baby down to sleep because she was so beautiful. It got so every time little Annie smiled at me like she knew I was her mama, I cried for an hour. Fish kept walking back and forth all nervous-like because he thought I was sick or something. But I was not. I was the happiest girl in the whole world. Here was this little tiny baby who I could tell already loved me more than I had ever been loved before.

When little Annie cried, which did not happen very much, she cried with her whole body like she was madder than a cat thrown in the river. You could tell she was strong as could be, because no little sickly child could have cried that loud and that long.

Miz Gray liked to hold little Annie, and she acted right proud that I'd named my baby after her. Sometimes I reckon she felt bad because she did not have little babies of her own. She never said anything, but when I'd see her put her cheek right next to little Annie's, I could tell Miz Gray felt powerful sad.

One day in April, Fish said most of the snow had melted away where the sun was shining, making the ground all warm. Miz Gray had worn a good path from the road through the woods, so anyone who wanted to find us could surely do that now. But we did not see Caswell or anybody else until one day Miz Gray came along, bringing the preacher with her.

On that fine, sunshiny spring day, Miz Gray waited and let

the preacher hold my baby first thing, like she did not want the preacher to see her acting sad. The preacher touched little Annie's cheek and touched what little bit of hair she had on her head, and then he said right away that my baby needed baptizing and he could do it that very day.

I looked at Fish to see if he thought this baptizing thing was a good idea, but he was watching the preacher hold my baby like he thought maybe the preacher would drop her on the ground. I was not sure Fish even heard what we were talking about.

"Fish, did you hear the preacher? About baptizing?"

Fish shrugged like it did not matter to him, but that was not a good enough answer for me. I'd keep asking questions until Fish said something like yes or no.

"Fish, is this baptizing something the Kickapoo do for new babies?"

Fish shrugged again. I was beginning to feel a bit put out that he was not willing to help, because he'd been practically my family for the whole winter, and I knew him a whole lot better than I knew the preacher.

"Preacher," I said. "I reckon I do not really know what this baptizing is, and maybe Fish does not know, either."

That's when Miz Gray jumped in and said it was of no consequence to the Indians unless they were Christians, which I do not think Fish ever thought of being, but that even if a little Indian baby got baptized by a Christian preacher, it would not hurt that baby at all and would not keep that little one from being a good Indian and believing all the things Indians believe. Miz Gray used a lot of big words I did not know, but I reckon she was mostly talking about the Great Spirit, leastways I thought so. I got too mixed up to even think about it anymore, so I decided to talk about leaving the river instead.

"Miz Gray," I said, "Fish and me and little Annie are fixing to move on out of here real soon. I do not think I can let my child grow up so close to Sangamon where Caswell and Mama are living."

The preacher looked at Miz Gray, and then he looked at Fish, and then he looked at little Annie, and then he looked at me. It almost seemed like he held my baby a little closer and even backed away from us a step. For a minute I thought he was going to turn tail and run into the woods.

"Where will you go?" he asked.

Fish walked closer to where the preacher stood with little Annie. He folded his arms across his chest and stood up straight. "My people crossed the great river," he said. "Jo Mae and the baby will be safe there."

"Live with the Indians?" The preacher said that like he thought it was a crazy notion and probably something Fish had put in my mind, but I went over to stand by Fish, and I did the same thing as him, putting my arms across my chest and standing up straight as a pole.

"That's what I'm aiming to do," I told the preacher.

"But you know you can stay with the preacher's parents in New Salem," Miz Gray said. "He told you that. In New Salem you'd have a good life. You'd be able to send your child to school. The Claymores can see that you get an education as well, learn a trade."

"And you'd be with people like yourself," the preacher said.

"Well, I do not know what that means, Preacher, since right now I feel a whole lot more like being an Indian than I do being in the middle of white people like the ones here in Sangamon. I cannot figure on any white folks being a whole lot different just because they live in a different town."

"Jo Mae, it would be different," said the preacher. "Your mother and brother will not know where you are. No one in New Salem will ever hurt you. My parents will be kind and do everything they can to help you."

"Jo Mae will choose," Fish said with a strong, deep voice that stopped the preacher and Miz Gray from saying one more word. I thought again about how it would be to live in a house with good people who would take care of me, and maybe I would have nice clothes and be able to take a bath every week, and little Annie could grow up with book learning and be somebody important like the schoolteacher.

But then I thought about what it would feel like if I had to watch Fish walking away all by himself to that great river. Knowing I might never see him again made my heart hurt so bad that right then and there, I knew I would not stay in New Salem, no matter how grand it was.

I reckon that talking about taking my baby and living with Fish and the Indians was going to cause more of a ruckus than talking about baptizing, so I up and asked the preacher to tell me what that was all about, so I could make up my mind. That's what he did, telling me all about original sin, which I did not rightly think little Annie could have.

But I thought that no harm would come of getting my baby to look even more beautiful in God's eyes, and surely that would also make her more beautiful in the Great Spirit's eyes, especially if Fish said his own Kickapoo prayer for new babies. Then little Annie would be safe from White Man's evil and Indian's evil, all at the same time. Then I got to thinking that maybe the preacher should do that baptizing for me too, because even though I felt a lot safer since Fish took me in, and I figured Fish had already told the Great Spirit that I needed help, I was sure Mama did not see fit to getting a preacher to pray over me when I was born. When I asked Miz Gray if I was baptized, she shook her head no. I figured she ought to know since she lived right there in Sangamon all the time. So the preacher said he would do that and said we should go down by the Sangamon

River, but before we could even move one step, there was a big yell from the woods.

"*Hallo, mon ami. J'arrive.*"

Everybody jumped and looked scared except Fish who hollered back, "Henri, *mon ami. Bienvenue.*"

I did not understand one word Fish said, so I looked where he was looking. There, coming out of the trees, was a man dressed in animal skins all sewed together so he looked like a big bear. I stared with my mouth hanging open when that man and Fish went running at each other and grabbed on like they were going to wrestle, and the man from the woods kissed Fish on both sides of his face. I almost had a coughing fit, because I'd never seen anything like that before.

They kept on talking away without saying any words that made sense, but then all of a sudden the man from the woods looked at Miz Gray and the preacher and bowed at the middle like a real gentleman, which made me laugh. He looked lots more like a big woolly animal. Then he started talking and had so much to say that I thought maybe he could talk near as much as me.

"I am Henri de Montagne, trapper and trader. You are Annie Gray from the village, are you not? I think perhaps we have met?"

Miz Gray stood there, stiff as a board, and did not even let a tiny smile onto her face, which was all pinched up like she took a bite out of a sour apple.

The trapper did not pay her any mind, but turned to the preacher, who still held my baby. He got closer to look at little Annie, all the while talking and talking. "You are a man of God, no? The dispenser of justice with an arm of fire?"

The preacher shook his head no, but I hollered out that he did too have an arm of fire, and he'd nearly killed my very own brother Caswell, about the wickedest man who ever lived, anyway the wickedest one I ever heard of.

The trapper looked at me like he thought I was the ugliest, or most beautiful, person in the whole world. I did not know which he was thinking. I wanted to go hide somewhere, but then he walked over to me and took his hand up to my face, and pushed my chin up nice as can be, and looked at me some more.

"And who are you, *ma petite*?"

"I am Jo Mae Proud and that is my baby the preacher is holding. He's going to baptize us both this very day and wash all the sin away, and then me and little Annie are leaving this place."

I looked at the preacher and decided I would not tell any more about us living with Fish, because I did not want to start up that talk again, especially now that there was one more grown-up person here to try and tell me what I should do.

The trapper took his hand away and stepped back when I said my name, and for once he did not have anything to say. For a while, it did not seem like anybody was going to say another word. I walked toward the river, figuring that folks who wanted to be part of the baptizing would come along.

Fish followed first. Next came the trapper walking close to the preacher, who was still carrying my baby, and trailing along at the back was Miz Gray. We were almost in a straight line, and we had our backs to the woods.

I guess everyone thought we were alone, but all of a sudden that old dog, who'd been sitting by the fire pit watching all the goings-on, growled and then barked and then growled some more. When we all looked to see what he was making a fuss about, we saw he was staring at the woods.

And standing there, right by the trees, were Mama and Caswell. I felt so sick I thought I would die. My heart started beating fast, and I couldn't breathe. Then I saw that Mama and Caswell were closer to the preacher and little Annie than I was.

I ran as fast as I could back up from the river.

At the same time, Caswell came running down from the woods like a big animal that's been shot full of arrows. The preacher stood there like he could not move. And he still did not move when Caswell grabbed little Annie right out of the preacher's arms and bumped and thrashed back to the trees like he was going to give my baby to Mama.

"Preacher," I screamed. "Get him!"

And still, that preacher did not do anything.

On my life, I could not figure out what was happening, but by then Fish and the trapper and me were all running toward Caswell, who got back to Mama and put my baby in her arms.

I thought Mama was going to take off running, but she never moved one step. She started talking to little Annie real soft, and for sure I thought she was even singing a little song. And then she moved her arms, rocking them back and forth.

I watched her to see what she was going to do all the time I was running, so I did not pay enough attention to Caswell. All of a sudden, he was coming in my direction, yelling my name and cursing something terrible.

"Preacher," I yelled again. "Kill him!"

But the preacher never even lifted his arm and tried. Right then, when I saw him standing there doing nothing, and I saw Fish coming as fast as he could to stand between me and this evil thing that wanted to do me harm, I knew for sure that I could not count on the preacher like I could count on Fish.

Just when Fish and the trapper got close enough to stand by my side, Miz Gray took three steps, which put her right between me and Caswell.

The exact minute Caswell tried to run past Miz Gray, she lifted up her skirt and pulled a big hunting knife out of a strap around her leg.

Caswell took one more step, and Miz Gray grabbed him

across the chest with one of her strong arms. I tried to run fast enough to grab that knife and kill that evil Caswell all by myself, but I was too slow. Miz Gray slashed her knife clear across Caswell's throat, and that was that.

She let go, and Caswell fell on the ground. I figured he was already dead as can be because he did not even twitch a finger. That old dog limped over and began to tear Caswell's throat wide open. Fish yelled and pulled the dog away.

It seemed like forever we stood there, staring down at the blood coming out of Caswell's neck. All of a sudden, I remembered little Annie.

Mama was still holding my baby, but now her face was white as new snow and bright pink spots marked her cheeks. Mama did not run away, and she did not cry. I walked over to her real slow so she would not get scared, and she waited until I got close. Then she put little Annie into my arms, and she turned and disappeared into the woods.

It was a wondrous thing to me that my baby was sleeping, and I reckon she'd been sleeping through everything that happened and never even knew that she'd been carried around by evil and could have died right then and there, if Caswell or Mama had wanted to kill her.

I turned around then to see what everyone else was doing.

The trapper stared into the woods like he'd seen a ghost.

Miz Gray was wiping down her knife with something white that looked like she might have tore it off her petticoat. She did not look like cutting Caswell's neck open bothered her one bit.

The preacher stood by Caswell's lump of a body, listening to something Fish was telling him. Fish shook his head and pointed toward the biggest tree that sat down by the river, way far from where we were standing. The preacher called the trapper over and pointed again. The three of them picked up Caswell and carried him down to the tree. They propped Caswell up so that he looked out over the river, which is a crazy thing to do, because he sure was not seeing anything. I could not figure why they'd do that.

I was not going to go along with baptizing me and little Annie with Caswell sitting there watching, but I guessed we would not have time for that anyway. I figured Mama would get some men from the town, and they would be coming for us. They'd be wanting to hang Miz Gray, so we'd all have to run away.

I was surprised when Miz Gray said she was going home, would not say a word about anything that happened in Fish's camp, and that whatever came of it was God's will.

Nothing we said would make her change her mind.

The trapper and Fish got busy then, scraping around on the ground where Caswell did all his bleeding. When they were done, there was not any sign of anything happening in the clearing around Fish's house and garden. The trapper said he'd ride into town after we were all gone, and tell folks that he'd found a body in the woods, and that he did not know how it got there or when.

They all made up their minds, without me having a say at all, that the preacher and his horse and Fish and me and little Annie would leave Sangamon right then with hardly anything except a bit of food and some blankets. We were going straight to New Salem, riding across the country instead of going on the roads. Anyone would expect us to go to St. Louis, so they'd be looking for us in the wrong place. No one would think of New Salem, the preacher said, because no one except us and Annie Gray knew he lived there when he was not traveling.

I saw the preacher looking at me while we were getting ready to leave. I knew he wanted to tell me why he did not raise his arm and throw more lightning at Caswell and strike him dead, but I did not care to hear what he was going to say. Maybe it was not up to the preacher to decide how God would get rid of evil creatures on this earth. Maybe God wanted to use Miz Gray to do what needed done.

I handed little Annie to Miz Gray and while she said her goodbyes, the preacher helped me get up on his spotty horse. Then Miz Gray kissed my baby on her head and handed her up to me to hold in my lap.

Miz Gray left first, walking into the woods, never giving a backward look or a wave.

Fish called the old dog, who I knew was going to slow down our travels, but I guess Fish would not leave the dog behind no matter what. Fish and the dog followed the preacher, who led the horse that little Annie and me rode on.

I looked back once at the Indian's camp, which had been my home for what seemed like a long time, and it hurt my heart to leave the best home I'd ever had. But I reckoned there was nothing I could do to change what happened, so I just looked at the trapper, who sat on a log by the fire pit and watched us, and I wondered what he was thinking.

When we reached the cool shade of the trees, I gave up trying to see the camp. I turned to look the way we were going, and I thought hard on what might happen next, and if little Annie would grow up safe, and what would become of Miz Gray if Mama told people what Miz Gray did to Caswell.

Thinking on that made me feel too scared, so I stopped. I looked up at the trees where I could see the tiny little leaf buds that were beginning to bust open. Breezes came flying out of nowhere and made the spots of sunlight on the tiny leaves jump around all shiny silver. Those spots were dancing around so happy-like, I could not help but look down at little Annie and smile.

"It's going to be a good life," I told her, and I swear she smiled back at me.

CHAPTER THIRTY-ONE:
THE INVESTIGATION

The Village of Sangamon wasn't big enough to have its own sheriff. What law existed was created and enforced by general agreement, at least when anyone cared enough to call a village meeting. If the town needed a lot of help, they called the army up from Jefferson Barracks near St. Louis, but that meant suffering through an invasion of soldiers who politely ate their way through folks' provisions. When it came to murder, however, someone would notify the federal marshal, if he could be found.

Small towns had their own way of dispensing justice, and even those as small as Sangamon could admit to an occasional hanging. For lesser crimes, a whipping might suffice. Most recently, the men of Sangamon had chased a peddler out of town and warned him never to return after the peddler lured one of Jeremiah's young daughters inside his wagon to see new bolts of calico prints and spindles of brightly colored ribbons. When the young lady emerged from the wagon with her bonnet askew and her sash untied, she was mortified to find her mother approaching to do a bit of shopping for herself.

This time Sangamon had a more serious crime on its hands: a murder no one seemed to have witnessed. A murder for which there were no—or perhaps too many—suspects.

And all of the townspeople in Sangamon watched their neighbors with a fearful curiosity.

And there were lanterns left burning through the night.

And there was more praying and teetotaling going on than was normal for even the holiest of towns.

At Mary Proud's insistence, Jeremiah and the other three men buried Caswell the same day they brought the body back to Sangamon. Jeremiah put his foot down about Caswell occupying the cemetery and placed the grave outside the fence. That way, he rationalized to Caswell's grieving mother, if the marshal showed up and needed to examine the corpse, the digging would be less likely to disturb the plots in the cemetery itself.

Jeremiah sent Sam and the saloonkeeper to St. Louis that same day. Two days later they returned to Sangamon with the federal marshal, who wanted to see the spot by the river where they'd found the body before he did anything else.

"Who lives out here?" the marshal asked.

The men who'd brought in the body exchanged glances and shrugged. "I live closest," said the saloonkeeper. "My place is on the edge of Sangamon, over by the burying grounds."

"I mean, there in the hut, under the trees," the marshal said.

"Well, that's Fish's place," said Sam. "Old Indian lives out here all alone."

"Heard he's gone," said Jeremiah.

"Wait," the marshal said. "You mean to tell me there was Injuns living out here and you let them get away?"

Jeremiah raised his hands in protest. "Not like that, Marshal. Only one old guy. He didn't make trouble, and he wasn't strong enough to kill a grown man, least not like this one that got killed."

The marshal shook his head in disgust. "Uh-huh. Who found the body?"

"Well, that would be the Frenchman," answered Sam. "But he's gone, too."

The marshal glowered at each of the men in turn as though

each bore the responsibility for aiding and abetting the escape of a whole band of murderers. After allowing several minutes to drift by in silence, he sighed. "This dead man got any kin?"

Jeremiah said, "There's Caswell's mama, Mary Proud. And his little sister. Jo Mae's her name."

"A kid? What would she know?"

"She used to go wading in the river," Jeremiah said. "Haven't seen her lately, but she might have been hanging around the Indian. Her and her ma both could tell you a thing or two about that fellow we buried, if they'd be willing. I'd sure enough start with the two of them."

Privately, between him and God, Jeremiah prayed Jo Mae did not show up again until the marshal had left town.

That afternoon, Jeremiah took the marshal up the muddy path that led to Mary Proud's cabin and knocked on her door. Mary's long hair tangled around her shoulders, and her white and blue gown was frayed at the seams and mud-stained around the hem. In contrast to the rest of her appearance, her hands were clean, the skin white.

Mary dismissed Jeremiah with one glance. She then leaned her head against the doorframe and said, "What do you want, Marshal?"

"It was your boy killed out by the river?"

"Yes."

"You also have a daughter? Dead man's sister?"

"Jo Mae? What do you want with her?"

"Got questions to ask her."

"She's gone. Didn't even come to her brother's burying."

"When did she leave?"

"Way back. Even before she birthed that baby, which I never saw, mind you, only heard about. Hasn't been here since last fall. September, I think."

"She has a baby? I thought she was a child."

"Marshal, she is a child, but she's one of the bad ones."

"Why'd she leave?"

Mary hesitated, then blurted out, "I sent her away. It was too shaming to have her here, growing big with child and everyone knowing she'd been rutting around with nearly every man in town. She's been nothing but trouble since the day she was born. I'm glad she's gone."

The frowzy woman then put her hand up to her head and closed her eyes. "I'm getting one of my headaches, Marshal. I have to get my medicine."

She abruptly shut the door in his face.

The marshal walked along the dirt road, spongy with spring snow melt. "Was it true? Did the child whore around with all the men in town?"

"Not that I've heard," Jeremiah said.

The marshal stopped and looked Jeremiah in the eye. "Do you know anything about the father of this girl's baby?"

"Not for certain. There are rumors."

"I assume those rumors involve her brother?"

Jeremiah didn't answer.

The marshal stood in silence and stared down the road toward the cemetery.

"You think there's any chance you'll figure out who killed Caswell?" Jeremiah asked.

"Hard to say. Seems like the folks most likely to do the deed, or to know who did it—the Injun, the Frenchman, and the girl—have disappeared. Who else in town should I be talking to?"

The marshal's conversation with Annie Gray provided very little additional information.

"Mr. Frost," she said, "why would you bring the marshal to see me? What could I possibly know about this horrible murder?"

"I'm talking to most everyone in town, ma'am. Mr. Frost here is showing me where folks live."

"Miss Gray, I did tell the marshal Caswell followed you all around town," Jeremiah said, "and the little girl worked in your garden."

"When she was younger, she did. Not so much in recent years. Then she up and vanished before winter came. I haven't seen her in months."

"And the boy?"

"Lightning hit him last summer, at a prayer meeting. After that he wasn't right."

"Why'd he pick you to follow around?"

"Not only me, Marshal. He trailed around after everybody. Peered in windows and such."

"Your windows?"

Annie shrugged. "Kept my shutters closed at night."

"Frost tells me an Injun lived out by the river, near where they found the boy's body."

"I couldn't tell you anything about that, Marshal."

"You didn't know this Injun?"

"Saw him around a time or two. Traded him a couple of hens a few years back."

The marshal paused, appeared to study Miss Gray's face like he wanted her to say more. He finally turned to Jeremiah. "Can you think of anyone else I should talk to?"

Annie Gray said, "What about Mary Proud?"

"Saw her before coming here."

"This . . . Injun you mentioned?"

"He's disappeared."

"What about the man who found the body?"

"The Frenchman? Gone."

"And you haven't seen the girl?"

216

"No," the marshal said. "You sure you don't know where she is?"

"No idea," Annie said. "No idea at all."

Even though he thought the dead man's sister might be a witness, the federal marshal did not expect her to be the killer. He figured the old Injun was the most likely culprit, considering the condition of Caswell's corpse. Who but an Injun would tear up a man's body that way? Lucky Caswell Proud hadn't been scalped as well.

Deputizing three of the town's men, the marshal and his posse rode out of town on the main road west, assuming the Injun would aim straight for the crossing at St. Louis before he turned north toward the reservations. The marshal couldn't tell a Kickapoo from a Sauk or a Winnebago from a Potawatomi. Didn't matter to him. He hated them all. He'd killed plenty of them during his time with the militia, back when they were hunting down Black Hawk. Taking out one more of the bloody breed wouldn't bother him one bit.

The marshal and his posse reached Decatur, only a few miles west of Sangamon, before sundown, only to find the town in an uproar. The bank—the only bank within fifty miles in any direction—had been robbed, the outlaws fleeing to the south. The marshal weighed the satisfaction to be gained in killing another savage, versus the reward offered by the bank's owner, and quickly made his choice. He dismissed the Sangamon posse and sent them home. The new and larger posse of Decatur citizens, led by the marshal, rode south.

The search for the Injun never resumed. The marshal never again thought about the unsolved murder of a village misfit no one would miss, except maybe his mother.

★ ★ ★ ★ ★

After Caswell had been buried and the federal marshal had come and gone, Mary still had not come to grips with the drastic changes in her life. She rarely ate, did not attempt to clean herself up, and went outside only to empty her chamber pot in the ditch behind the cabin.

One day, however, Mary got out of bed and hung a pot of water on the fireplace hob. She rummaged in the old leather chest she'd lugged from Pennsylvania to Dearborn to Sangamon, and pulled out a musty blue gown she had not worn since Henri de Montagne left. She selected white undergarments edged with lace, and blue ribbons for her hair. She took her silver hairbrush to her tangled hair and brushed it until it hung smooth and straight to the middle of her back.

When the water in the pot was warm, Mary heaved it free of the hook and hefted it up to sit on the table. With a piece of cloth torn from an old tattered gown, and a piece of lye soap Annie had given her years ago, Mary washed her body and rinsed it free of the harsh cleaner. She dipped half of the warm water out and set it aside, then dunked her head in the pot and scrubbed her hair until her scalp burned. She poured the remaining water over her head to rinse out the soap.

Finally, dressed in her fine blue dress, she tied her hair back with the ribbons. She then searched again through the contents of her old chest and found a brooch of red and blue stones and a tiny bottle of rose water. She pinned the brooch to her bodice, and patted the rose water on her neck.

Taking a deep breath to quell her anxiety, Mary opened her door and stepped outside. She stood still, breathing in the scent of late spring, then squared her shoulders and strode toward the schoolhouse. It was early, and children were still inside, reciting the alphabet in a singsong fashion as though bored to death. Mary waited, leaning against the outside wall as she listened.

When finally the children ran past her, scattering in all directions, Mary stepped inside and approached the schoolteacher. What she wanted, she said, was to know the names of the parents of any children who would benefit from extra schooling. The schoolteacher obliged.

Mary called on seven families that day. She received commissions from three families to tutor their children. She took the gold nugget, given to her years ago by Henri de Montagne, to Jeremiah Frost and enlisted his help in ordering primers for children, books for her own pleasure, and two pairs of reading glasses. She had enough credit left over to last years. She purchased a broom, a new kettle, and two calico sunbonnets, as well as cornmeal and sugar.

By the time Mary's father passed through Sangamon a second time, Mary's life had changed. She welcomed him back with a warm embrace, and asked if he could help her repair her cabin before he left.

Annie Gray took up the care of her animals and prepared her land for her spring garden and summer crops, working hard and spending little time in the village. After a few months, when the new hens she'd purchased began laying, Annie made a casual call on Mary Proud to deliver eggs. Mary's appearance had changed so drastically, Annie hardly recognized her.

In her clean gown, with carefully groomed hair, Mary stood at her door with a broom in her hand. She accepted Annie's offering with an aloof expression, which she did not attempt to soften with a smile or any word except a simple, "Obliged." She did not introduce the tall white-haired man who sat near the hearth.

With no mention made of Caswell, or of Jo Mae, and with no more visits from the federal marshal, Annie renewed her normal activities with confidence.

CHAPTER THIRTY-TWO:
JO MAE IN NEW SALEM

It took almost four whole days to get to that New Salem that preacher took us to. I got to ride the horse and carry little Annie, while all that time Fish and the old dog and the preacher walked along like they were used to walking. Fish and the preacher never said anything about their feet hurting, but I know they did because I remember that long walk from the Hobart's farm back to Fish's camp.

We'd stop for a while when it got dark and eat a bit of Fish's dried meat and Miz Gray's dried apples, and then try to sleep on the ground, but we'd get cold right to our bones. Up we'd get before long and start walking around to get warm. Preacher figured if we were going to walk to keep warm we might as well be on our way.

I reckon I was never so glad to see a place as I was to see the preacher's New Salem. It was way bigger than Sangamon with lots more cabins and they looked new as could be. There were three general stores, and down at the very end of the town was a big house made of real boards. The preacher said those boards were cut from trees, which I could not hardly believe, but he said he'd take me down to the sawmill by the river and I could see for myself. He said the screechy noises we heard came from that very sawmill where a great big saw was cutting up a tree.

Another thing in that town that I never did see before was a little cabin that the preacher said was the post office for getting mail. Then, of course, he had to tell me what mail was, and that was another thing to figure on because I never thought about folks having other folks in faraway places and wanting to send letters telling them all about what was happening to them. I thought maybe someday I could write a letter to Mama. But maybe she would not care about what happened to me and little Annie.

About the time I started to feel sad that Mama probably was happy I took off, a tall man with long arms and legs walked right out of that little post office and went straight to the preacher and shook his hand, and they talked about elections and stuff and laughed like they were the best of friends, and all the while that tall man looked us over—Fish, Old Dog, me, and little Annie. The preacher said later that the man was the postmaster and his good friend, and that he wanted to help us if he could.

When we got to the cabin where Preacher's mama and papa lived, I could not believe my eyes. It was bigger than any log cabin I had ever seen, and it had a little floor sticking out in front of it, and a rocking chair sat right there outside and some pots with flowers. Preacher told us to follow him inside, so Fish and Old Dog, and me holding Annie, walked right in like we were walking into our own home. But it sure did not look much like my home with Mama and Caswell.

The room we were standing in was big and had two fireplaces and a fine big table with some chairs, and none of it looked dirty or rickety like it was going to fall down. There were doors every which way, and I could see beds with quilts on them, and they were every color you could think about. About the time when I wondered if one of those beds might be where me and Annie could sleep, a lady rushed in the door and stopped sudden-like and stared at all of us like she'd found her cabin full of snakes.

"Mother," Preacher said, "I've brought some folks here who

need our help."

Well, Preacher's mama did not pay him any mind. She grabbed up the tail of her apron and waved it, hollering, "Shoo, shoo," and moving toward the dog, and it was like Miz Gray trying to chase her chickens out of her garden. That old dog stuck his tail between his legs and bent his poor old head down like he was ashamed of himself, and he scooted on out the door quicker than a scared rabbit.

After the dog ran outside, Preacher's mama turned around and put that hard look on Fish. Her lips were smashed together, and all around her mouth was white, and I think she looked about as mean as Mama always did right before she'd slap me hard. I got scared Miz Claymore was going to slap Fish like that. I put out my hand, but before anything else happened, Fish stood up straight and pushed his chin out and crossed his arms over his chest and walked right out that door. As he walked by Miz Claymore, she gave his elbow the tiniest push, and then she grabbed up the tail of her apron again and wiped both her hands so hard you'd have thought they were covered with chicken innards.

When she turned that scary look on me, I figured out why Fish went right out the door.

"You wanting me to take my baby outside?" I asked her.

She didn't say a word to me but turned around to look eye-to-eye with the preacher. "Why have you brought them here? Surely you don't expect—"

"They need help, Mother. You've assisted many needy people over the years."

"No filthy Indians," Miz Claymore shouted. "Those heathens murdered women and children. They took scalps. If we hadn't fled Galena, they'd have killed us as well.

"And this girl," she said. "You've brought me a half-wild, uneducated girl with a baby? Don't tell me this bastard is yours."

"Of course not. Mother, I told you about the girl the last time I came home. You seemed quite sympathetic—"

But I did not wait to hear whatever more the preacher said because I figured if Miz Claymore could say such awful things about Fish and could call my baby Annie a bastard, then she was not a kind person at all. I looked back at the preacher one time and he was staring at his mama like he did not even know who she was, and I reckon maybe he did not.

I took little Annie and walked out to the road where Fish stood like a post with that old dog lying by his feet.

"Were you waiting for me?" I asked.

Fish did not say anything.

Before I had a chance to say one more word, the preacher hurried out of the cabin. "Come back inside," he said, looking me right in the eye but not looking at Fish at all. "My mother has reconsidered."

But I did not know what that meant so I asked him, and he told me, and then I said, "Fish, too?"

"She'll not allow that. I'll find another place for Fish to stay."

"I reckon not, Preacher." And I meant to stick by my words, no matter what the preacher said to try and make me change my mind.

That night Fish and the old dog and me and little Annie all slept on the floor of the post office, and the postmaster brought us blankets and so much food that we were ready to bust after eating it all. He even said we could stay as long as we wanted, but Fish and me decided we were going to move on, because maybe New Salem was not going to be so nice after all.

We were still way far from that big river the preacher called the Mississippi, and after getting on the other side, we'd have to walk a long time to find the Kickapoo, but that's what Fish wanted to do. I figured that whatever Fish thought was good for him would be good for me and Annie.

Preacher did get us some help from his daddy and from the postmaster. They got us a mule and a little cart, and they filled the cart up with blankets and all kinds of things to eat and some jugs for water and a little kettle for cooking. Preacher's daddy was a mite more kind than Miz Claymore was. He even shook hands with me and Fish, and he smiled at little Annie and tried to tickle her under the chin to make her laugh.

But I reckon Miz Claymore made the rules about who goes and who stays in that big fancy cabin of hers, and I did not think she'd change her mind just because Mr. Claymore was a nice man.

Soon as we had all those things, Fish and I were ready to go. I turned around one time and waved at the preacher. He was standing in the middle of the road, watching us, and in all those times I had seen the preacher, I had never seen him look that sad, almost like he was going to cry right there. I quickly looked away, because I did not want to feel sad on this day.

When we finally came upon that river everybody said was so big, I stood there looking at it, because I could not figure how anyone could ever get to the other side, which I could hardly even see from where I was standing. Then I saw that teensy cabin out on the river. It had a big flat floor all around it, like outside Miz Claymore's cabin, and it got closer and closer. A man stood on the edge, sticking a long pole in the water, and slow as can be that thing was coming right to where we were standing.

"That's how we're going to the other side?" I asked Fish.

"Huh," he said back. And I knew that meant yes.

The minute that flat boat was pushed away from the land, I sat down and started to cry. I cried so hard and so long I thought maybe I wasn't going to ever stop. But I did, and when I looked up at Fish, I saw he was standing close by, looking at the other side of the river getting closer and closer. "I'm done crying now."

"Huh," was all he said, but he touched my shoulder and took little Annie in his arms while I got up and waited until we could walk onto dry land again.

Most of the time we were walking, I had Annie tucked in a pouch thing Fish made from one of his old deerskin shirts. It hung around my neck and over one shoulder, and little Annie would swing back and forth if I walked, or jiggle up and down if I rode in the cart. She did not seem to mind the swinging and the jiggling too much. I guess she was growing just fine because she was getting harder to tote around. Sometimes my neck and back hurt something fierce from carrying her so long.

We kept going every day and my legs got strong and my neck and back quit hurting. I'd go barefoot if the road was nice and smooth or if the grass alongside was soft and there were no thorns or nettles. After a time, my blisters were all gone and the skin on my feet was tough as deer hide.

All the time I was walking, I thought about the things that had gone on since I was a little girl, and about things that might happen now that Annie and I were going to be with Fish. With all that thinking, I did not talk so much as I did before, and I stopped crying so much, so Fish could tell that my spirit was doing fine and he let me be. There were some days that we did not talk all day long, and we did not mind at all.

There was something mighty peaceful about my days once I knew for sure I was all done with wishing Caswell dead.

ABOUT THE AUTHOR

Pat Stoltey is the author of two crime fictions, *The Prairie Grass Murders* and *The Desert Hedge Murders*. Standalone thriller, *Dead Wrong,* was a finalist in the 2015 Colorado Book Awards. A short story, "Three Sisters of Ring Island," appeared in the 2014 anthology *Tales in Firelight and Shadow.*

A former accounts payable manager, Pat began writing seriously after retirement. She has lived in Illinois, Indiana, Oklahoma, and the south of France, but now she's a happy resident of Northern Colorado with her husband, Katie Cat, and Sassy Dog.

Learn more about Pat at: http://patriciastolteybooks.com.

The employees of Five Star Publishing hope you have enjoyed this book.

Our Five Star novels explore little-known chapters from America's history, stories told from unique perspectives that will entertain a broad range of readers.

Other Five Star books are available at your local library, bookstore, all major book distributors, and directly from Five Star/Gale.

Connect with Five Star Publishing

Visit us on Facebook:
   https://www.facebook.com/FiveStarCengage

Email:
   FiveStar@cengage.com

For information about titles and placing orders:
   (800) 223-1244
   gale.orders@cengage.com

To share your comments, write to us:
   Five Star Publishing
   Attn: Publisher
   10 Water St., Suite 310
   Waterville, ME 04901

CS

FRANKLIN SQUARE PUBLIC LIBRARY
19 LINCOLN ROAD
FRANKLIN SQUARE, NY 11010
516-488-3444

JAN 1 1 2018